SATURDAY NIGHT,
TONY GOES DANCING.

"Tony?" The girl was about eighteen. Her name: Annette. Her eyes were fixed on Tony. She called his name again.

"Yeah," Tony said in a bored way and slowly stood up.

"Whaddya mean . . . yeah?" Annette demanded.

"I mean, yeah, I'll dance with you. But you are definitely not my dream girl."

He left her standing at the table and walked directly to the dance floor. By the time he had chosen his spot and turned, she was right where she was supposed to be with her arms slightly raised and held out to him, ready.

"Let's dance," Tony said . . .

Paramount Pictures Presents
A Robert Stigwood Production

John Travolta
Karen Gorney

"SATURDAY NIGHT FEVER"

Screenplay by
Norman Wexler

Based Upon a Story by
Nik Cohn

Produced by
Robert Stigwood

Directed by
John Badham

In Color
A Paramount Picture

Soundtrack album available
on RSO Records

23" x 35" full-color poster
of the cover photograph
available wherever
posters are sold

Saturday Night Fever

A Novelization by
H. B. Gilmour

Based on a Screenplay by
Norman Wexler

From a Story by
Nik Cohn

SATURDAY NIGHT FEVER
A Bantam Book | December 1977

ISBN 0–553–11565–0

Published simultaneously in the United States and Canada

Bantam Books are published by Bantam Books, Inc. Its trade-
mark, consisting of the words "Bantam Books" and the por-
trayal of a bantam, is registered in the United States Patent
Office and in other countries. Marca Registrada. Bantam
Books, Inc., 666 Fifth Avenue, New York, New York 10019.

PRINTED IN THE UNITED STATES OF AMERICA

*For the two Mars
and the one and only Jess.*

Saturday Night
Fever

Prologue

Everything is changing. The rainbow spray of lights across the disco floor captures rapture, splashing from face to waist to hands carving rhythms in the multicolored space. The blinding, bouncing white spots hit the tiers of tables behind the dance floor, freeze the speed-driven action for a second, then release their hostages contemptuously.

On the other side of the room Bernie, the DJ, is high in his control booth, high on his fantasy of control. He plays the music you move to. He makes you go crazy or slow. And, every once in awhile, he howls through his mike so you don't forget just who is the wiz of 2001 Odyssey Ballroom.

But, down at the first and best tier, ringside, the Faces know who really owns the place. Ask them and they'll probably laugh or lay you out. Who's the disco king? Whaddaya kidding? Tony. Tony Manero.

Bobby C. is sitting at the only Reserved table with his pad and pencil out. He's sketching a gum-popping, heavy-knockered chick a table away. Her chewing is synched to the music. Her eyes are half-lids. Her mouth motion says she's on speed; her lids say 'ludes. Her breasts say Women's Lib has reached Bay Ridge, Brooklyn—but they lie. Bobby C. can spot the golden Jesus cross hanging right between those big, lying, braless boobs. And where there's a cross there's a stiff penalty for penetration. Oh sweet Jesus, Bobby C. remembers miserably. What the hell's he going to do about Pauline? Hot, dumb, ugly as they come—and probably pregnant—Pauline. Crosses! Catholic broads! They should cross their legs.

But ask Bobby C.: Who's the king of 2001 Odyssey Ballroom? Who gets pick of the pussy? Who always gets a chance to dance in the backseat? Ask Double J. He's sitting next to Bobby C., looking for action—always. His young scarred fist is wrapped around a glass and he's wishing it was a neck or ass or something to tear into. Double J.'s meaner than he's pretty, and that makes him mighty mean. Ask Joey, the pug. He's built like a fireplug, only the kind you definitely do not piss on. Ask any of the Faces sprawled around the only Reserved table—Double J., Gus the slightly round clown, Joey or Bobby C.

It's Saturday night and everything's changing behind the splashing disco lights, behind the pills, poppers, and vodka; behind the music and sights of frenzied tits and asses Hustling; behind the pants riding cherry high. And he's moving among them, Tony Manero, who could have it all for a dance.

Ask anyone who comes to 2001 steady. Hey, who's the tough-cool always gets the best table? How come the girls ask him to dance? So he's pretty when he smiles; so he moves slow and talks low . . . and he glows, man, out on the floor. When he dances he's gone and even who he's with doesn't exist. He's just this flowing, flawless body. Like a ripple of music, like a spray of light. He's Tony Manero. Only 18. The disco king. And while he's dancing, everything's changing. Even the day.

It's just about midnight. Saturday to Sunday is one beat away. And sometimes Tony can dance so fine and hard he forgets that everything around him is changing.

I

Saturday

For a couple of years when he was younger, the counterman worked in his uncle's pizza parlor on East 86th Street in Manhattan. That was during the sixties, when there were anti-war demonstrations every other day. Kids, dressed in workshirts and jeans, would rush out of line to his window for a slice. They were rich people's kids. They had rich accents. And while they ate their pizzas, they didn't talk too much about whose brother became a body count in Nam the week before. It was all Love and Peace, Dylan and Baez, Pigs and Flower Power.

The next day, sometimes the same day, the other side would march. They were workers. The papers called them blue-collar workers or hard hats, but they dressed decently. They didn't wear work clothes like the kids who didn't work. They had flag pins in their lapels and when they stopped at the window for a slice, you could understand them. Their language was rough as their hands. Their accents were familiar. They could have come from Queens or the Bronx, Staten Island or Brooklyn. They were New York, all right. But not Manhattan.

A decade later, here he was working in a pizza parlor on 86th Street again. But not Manhattan. He was back in Bay Ridge and it was like the sixties never happened to Brooklyn.

He swiped at the counter with a damp cloth before resting his elbows on the Formica. He stared out

3

the window at the street. Inflation, depression—nothing ever slowed the flow of shoppers on Saturday afternoon. Week after week, the same pinched-faced women passed, trying to mug-proof their purses by squeezing them between their scrawny arms and breasts. The same buxom, wide-assed women, too, trying to save a nickel by dragging their own shopping bags from home. And the young ones, the almost-women, in whose bodies, however lush or slim, were the ugly little secrets of their mothers: wrinkles and varicose veins hiding under the flawless skin; breasts and bottoms held high by muscles that might hang in there for another five years, ten if they were lucky. The women. The beer-burly men squinting out of the bars; some still wore flags in their lapels on Sundays. The rag-assed kids—so many, the Pope ought to come down and personally congratulate the neighborhood.

Through the flow of Saturday shoppers, the counterman spotted the boy. How many kids did you see like that? The brown leather jacket, the cheap pants, the platform shoes—they were a dime a dozen. But the way the boy moved, sauntering down 86th like he had nowhere to go and nothing to do but decide whether to buy the block or not. There was something about Tony Manero that always made the counterman smile.

Tony had black hair, olive skin, full lips, a slightly crooked smile, and teeth so white, so dazzling, you'd swear they were false. Like magazine teeth, money teeth. Like Manhattan. But three generations Brooklyn Italian, that's what he really looked liked. That's what he was.

Built good, too. Of course, he was a little shorter than he looked in those funny platform shoes. All the kids seemed to go for them these days. Everyone wanted to stand tall. Some could. Some couldn't. The Manero kid, though, he had the right body and moves to make the make-believe height look real. Watching him swinging down 86th anyone could tell that if the shoes hadn't given him the extra inch, he'd have found some other way to get it.

The counterman turned from the window and began to carve up the large pie that lay on the marble slab behind him. Tony came in; he was ready.

"Two or three?" he asked, smiling.

"Two for now."

He nodded, scooped two slices of pizza onto the wooden oven shovel and popped them in to heat.

"Your boss should see how hard you work." With a toss of his head, he indicated the can of paint Tony was carrying.

The boy's eyes sparked angrily for a moment. Then, realizing that the remark had been merely conversational, that it held no threat, he relaxed and grinned. He paid for the pizzas, piled the steaming slices one on top of the other, picked the gallon can of paint up by its wire handle and turned to leave. He'd devoured half the double-deckered slices before he even hit the street.

That kind of hunger a hundred pizzas don't satisfy, the counterman thought. And, for a split second, he almost understood what it was he liked about the boy. Then he shook his head and laughed at himself. He remembered how his mother, God rest her soul, always used to call him the Philosopher.

Tony made a ball of the grease-stained pizza napkin. He twirled and jump-shot the crumpled paper over the heads of shoppers toward a wire trash can near the curb. Two girls in matching fake leather jackets whirled around indignantly to see where the napkin had come from. When they spotted Tony, the short one squeezed her friend's arm frantically. "He's the one," she whispered. "Oh Donna, I'm dying. From 2001. You know. The one from the disco."

"Oh yeah," Donna said. She tossed her long black hair back grandly, but her face betrayed her excitement. "He really does look like Al Pacino," she gasped. "Honest to Christ. In daylight, even."

Tony heard. He was very satisfied. But he denied

them a glance. Later, maybe, he'd nod at them if they showed up at 2001. Maybe. Maybe not. The one with the long hair was a sloppy dancer.

He turned his back on them and checked out the clothes in Shirtown's window. There was one striped shirt among a multitude of shimmering jungle prints. It was different, but dynamite. Shades of soft blue with a wide disco collar and tapered just right. Good cut. He opened the door of the haberdashery and called to the salesman who was standing just inside.

"Hey, that striped one—$27.50—you got it in extra-large?"

"You take extra-large, we got extra-large. Even if we have to change the tag." The salesman did not sound thrilled.

"Yeah, all right," Tony said. Scowling, he shut the door. He didn't quite slam it. Just pulled it hard enough to match the smart-assed salesman's level of politeness.

Back on the street, he made a point of not looking at the shirt again, but he was thinking about it. Not the money so much, but what really mattered: how it would move. He tried to imagine the feel of it against his chest and shoulders when he danced. He tried to gauge the leeway his arms would have for liquid motion. The look, like gift-wrapped second skin. He liked dressing well. Covering his body just right. He believed you had to. You had to show respect for your body. It was like owning a pearl-handled gun or a perfectly balanced knife. The holster you chose, the hand-tooled sheath—they had to be worthy of the weapons they encased. That shirt, too, it would have to fit and ride just right because Tony Manero's body was, after all, his weapon. He was a killer. A star. Like Bruce Lee. Like, yeah, Al Pacino.

The long-haired girl wasn't the first to notice that. Just after *Godfather II* came out, he and some of the other Bay Ridge Faces had gotten stoned and wound up in some disco in Staten Island. A low place. Strictly home turf stuff and hostile. He'd danced anyway. He'd done a few unpolished flash routines—nothing to turn heads at 2001, but in that hole the locals fell back A-fucking-mazed. Then this little chick came over and stared up into his face. She just stood there and stared and finally he said, "Hey, what you want?" and she said, "Kiss me!" and he did and she almost passed out.

"Oooooo," she swooned. "I just kissed Al Pacino."

He laughed. He knew she was nuts, but he also knew she really meant it. It was mindblowing. This weird little chick coming up to him, seeing him like that. He knew she was nuts, but it got to him. She really *saw* him. Al Pacino!

In the middle of the block, Tony put the gallon can of paint on his head and stood tough and still. A killer, a star. But the girl in the platform shoes whose path he was blocking, the one he'd caught turning to look at him a minute before, just blushed and walked around him.

A few feet from Bayside Paints, he began to run furiously. Through the store window Dan Fusco's eager-beaver face peered vigilantly. He was wiping his glasses with a handkerchief. When Tony appeared, Fusco popped the glasses quickly back onto his nose and, flailing his arms wildly, tried to signal through the window to the boy.

Tony's hand was already on the front doorknob when he spotted Fusco. His instinct was to crack up. Fusco looked so crazy, soft-eyed and desperate, waving like a mad man. But Tony held back the laugh. Fusco—stocky, bespectacled, nervous wreck that he was—was still the boss. The owner. He deserved something for that. He owned something. He had this huge, busy store—Bayside Paints—which was jumping today with all the weekend painters and patchers coming in for their supplies. And if it wasn't for Dan Fusco, there wouldn't be too much sauce on the pasta these days. Not at home, at hotshot Frank Manero's house. Not with the big man laid off and everyone depending on Tony to bring home the bucks.

So, Tony owed Dan Fusco. He didn't have to love him, but he wouldn't laugh in his face either. Although, if the clown didn't start making sense with those hand signals, Tony might just not be able to hold it back much longer.

Finally, Fusco got it under control enough to wave his thumb in a backward motion and Tony nodded his head and ran around the block to the rear door of the paint store.

Fusco was waiting for him when he entered. In the chaos of the small utility room that also served as an office, Fusco was leaning up against the desk, looking almost as winded as Tony was supposed to be.

Tony took his leather jacket off and hung it carefully on the wall hook.

"What'd he charge you?" Fusco demanded, tossing his work jacket to him.

"Seven dollars. Ninety-eight cents."

The jacket was one of those loose-fitting, rough cotton ones, the kind that doctors and druggists wore . . . or janitors. Tony liked it, though. He liked the concern it implied for his street clothes, and the professional look of it. He slipped into the jacket while Fusco did a slow burn, only not so slow.

"The bastard!" Fusco's eyes were almost as out of control now as his hands had been at the front window. "You know why he had the nerve to charge you that? Because it's Saturday, that's why. He knows I'm probably up to my ass here and that I ain't got the time. . . . But wait. Just wait til he runs out of something. Go. Go on. They're piling up out there."

Tony picked up the gallon can and headed for the front. He breezed through the aisles, putting on steam as he approached his customer.

"Sorry it took so long. I had to get it from our reserve stock, know what I mean, sub-basement."

He rang up the sale. Then another. He raced up the sliding ladder for a pint of varnish, then down and through the tidy aisles for a roller and tray. A fat man tapping his fingers impatiently on the counter slid a color-sample chip at him. He looked at it and nodded.

"Hey, don't you want the number?" the fat man called as Tony headed for the rear of the store.

"I know it," he said.

The man seemed annoyed.

It was time to put a little flash into the act, Tony decided. It was time to knock this jerk-off out with a flawless performance. He kicked the ladder ahead of him, slowed it with his toe, and was up and at the right can of paint before the ladder stopped rolling. Paint can held high in one hand like a movie picture waiter's tray, he straddled the ladder and slid down.

"Carnival Red. Benjamin Moore, 13323," he said, presenting the can with a flourish.

Fusco passed behind him as he finished ringing up the sale. The old man was beaming. He clapped Tony on the back. "Atta way. The customers like that. The way you run up that ladder."

The next customer wanted some brushes.

"How much painting you going to do?" Tony asked him.

"After these two rooms, I wouldn't paint my wife's ass purple," the man said. "And it could use a paint job."

"Oh yeah. What color is it now?" Tony asked impassively.

Immediately, the man's face turned grim and challenging. He pinned Tony with a dark look; dark tending toward dangerous.

"You wanna know what color my wife's ass is?" the man said menacingly.

Tony smiled his patient lop-sided smile. "You brought it up," he reminded the customer. People who were always ready to make a big deal out of nothing bothered him. For starters, he didn't understand them. Personally, he never fussed. If someone started flipping out in front of him, like cursing or screaming or threatening, nine times out of ten Tony would turn his back on them and quietly start walking. If he were at 2001 Odyssey now, he'd walk. But he was at Bayside Paints. So he smiled with his mouth and disappeared behind his eyes.

Finally, the customer decided that Tony was just being friendly. He relaxed. He let the glowering pinch out of his face and smiled back.

"Shit," the man said like a good natured John Wayne, "Actually my wife's ass ain't got no color. Just stripes. Them stretch stripes. Hell, maybe I oughta paint it. What about them brushes?"

"For the rooms—or your wife's ass?"

Perplexed and offguard now, the man replied mournfully, "The rooms. Her ass—I could do with a toothbrush."

"Second display rack behind you," Tony directed icily. His smile was gone. He had suddenly tried to imagine his father talking that way about his mother—to a stranger, to an absolute stranger, a guy in a store who he didn't know from a hole in the ground. It was impossibe to imagine, thank God.

At six, Fusco finally locked the front door and turned the Open sign around. He looked beat. His work jacket was limp, frayed and dirty around the wrists.

They were in the utility room together. Tony took his leather jacket from the wall peg.

"Uh, Mr. Fusco," he began.

Fusco pulled his tie off. He had to squint before he could focus on Tony's face. He was too tired to even say, "What?" He just looked up from under his eyebrows, straining, it seemed, to keep a steady fix on Tony. His patient, wide-eyed stare implored the boy to ask his question, get it over with.

"Mr. Fusco, can I get an advance?"

Firmly, Fusco replied: "Payday is Monday."

The shirt. Shades of icy blue stretching across his shoulders and chest, smooth and cool, opened maybe three, four buttons down so his medal would flash in the changing lights. He looked at Fusco who was gray, whose face and shirt and skin and, probably even underwear, were gray. How could he make someone like Fusco understand what only a Face could ever know? How could he describe the ecstasy, the necessity, of dancing precisely in precisely the right shirt? No way.

"I know payday's Monday . . ." There was an edge to his voice that made him sick. A Face didn't whine, ever. The rules, Tony, reminded himself. He took a breath, not so you could see it, but inside. He took a cleansing, calming breath . . . the kind he'd take before turning his back on an argument. "I know payday's Monday," he said again, testing the adjustment. "Everyplace else it's Friday or Saturday."

"And they're broke on Monday. Right?" Fusco challenged. "Boozing, whoring, pissing away the money all weekend. This way, paid on Monday, you've got money all week. You can save a little. Build for the future."

"Fuck the future," Tony said.

Fusco shook his head, sadly. Then, he smiled but not with his tired eyes.

"No, Tony. You can't fuck the future. The future fucks you. It catches up with you and fucks you." By way of reprieve, he offered, "If you haven't planned for it."

Tony took another breath. He could feel his lungs expanding, pushing against the weight that Fusco and all the gray people were always trying to lay on it.

"Tonight's the future," he said surely. "Tonight, and I'm planning for it. There's a shirt I've got to buy."

"Sorry, Tony." Fusco ended the discussion. "No exceptions." He unlocked the back door and let Tony out.

On the street, Tony could feel the adrenalin starting to flow. Whatever happened inside the store, when the door closed, he stepped out into Saturday night.

He dashed over to Shirtown. He could hardly bear to look at the shirt in the window. He just saw the color, knew it was there, caught a glance of the hand-printed price card propped on the floor next to it. Then he opened the door. The bored salesman was folding sweaters.

"You guys do layaway?" Tony asked him.

"So long as it don't turn into a twenty-year mortgage."

Tony pulled a five out of his wallet. "Okay, here's a five down on the blue striped in the window." He laid the bill on the counter next to the sweaters and turned to go.

"Hey, wait for a receipt."

"I trust you," Tony told him. He had to get out now. He had to get ready.

"Don't," the salesman called after him. "Do me a favor, don't trust me."

Moving on the balls of his feet, as if he were dribbling a ball up the court, he headed up 86th Street. At the pizza parlor, he held three fingers up signaling through the window. By the time he was inside, the counterman was shoveling the slices into the oven.

"You had two, two hours ago. This'll make five."

"What's the bitch?" Tony said offhandedly. "You pissed that you ain't working on commission?"

"Naw. I'm just jealous," the counterman laughed, " 'cause you got such an outstanding figure."

Tony blinked. Was this guy calling him a faggot? No fuss. Deep breath. No hassles.

The counterman sensed the confusion. "Hey, I was kidding around, you know. I just never saw no one burn up the calories like you. Here," he slid the three slices over the counter. "Enjoy 'em while you can."

Tony piggybacked the pizzas as usual.

"You are one real hungry boy," the counterman murmured as Tony left the store.

Down the block, leisurely smoking and leaning against a store window, a Puerto Rican boy noticed Tony gobbling the triple-stacked pizzas. He couldn't care less. But, carelessly, he had let his dark eyes touch Tony's.

As he drew near the boy, Tony tilted his head

the way he'd seen this dude tilt his in one of those Italian Westerns he'd caught on late night TV.

"*Hombre*," he said, sinisterly, "you will die."

The Puerto Rican kid's face registered quick shock, then hovered between fear and anger. He pinched his cigarette between his thumb and forefinger, ready to fling it in self defense.

"When?" he gasped.

"Later," said Tony very, very softly.

"Later, when?" the kid implored. "Later, what?"

Tony never looked at him again. "When the clock strikes . . . when the fucking clock strikes the fucking mouse . . ." he drawled into the air. Drawled, slurred it just right. He had turned 86th Street into a dusty no man's land where strangers leaning against store windows would never get the draw on him. Just like that dude in the Western. A killer, a star.

Frank Manero was a big man. Six feet tall, over 200 pounds. The calluses on his hands could probably compete with those of the best board breakers at the Martial Arts School. He'd built those calluses week by week, over twenty-five years, shoveling, hauling, handling bricks, cement, asphalt—you name it. Twenty-five years a construction worker. One goddamn year a bum.

Frank Manero had been laid off and it hurt. Flo, his wife, never rode him about it or, thank God, gave him the kind of pep talks that went down like charity ward gruel, but he knew, he noticed, that recently things had begun to change. It would have been hard for him to put his finger on it, but little things, attitudes, were different. Of course, he'd been hanging around where he didn't belong. He'd been on his ass in the house when he should have been out there in the weather. That got on his nerves. Maybe it was starting to get on her nerves, too. But he was still the boss.

Mama didn't say nothing about nothing. Sometimes he wanted to take her tiny white hands into his

and just kind of ask her what she thought. Did she
think he was a loafer? Did she understand how it was
eating his guts out to do nothing? He glanced at his
mother now. She was in the living room, sitting
straight as always, clutching that rosary Frank Jr.
had given her for Christmas. Her dress was black,
always. The little lace collar was crisp as spring, white
as her hair. Amazing. Fifty-three years she'd been
in this country and never spoke a word of English yet.

Frank   shivered   suddenly.   The newspaper
propped before him rippled. Sweet Jesus, he thought,
he'd almost crossed himself. Why? If he had to answer
truthfully it was probably because he'd looked at the
old lady and thought: God in heaven, don't let her
die without seeing me back on my feet again; without
her seeing me working again and earning a decent
living like a man.

Linda, his daughter, came out of the kitchen
with Flo. "Papa, I gotta set now," she reminded him.
He folded his newspaper and handed it to Flo, but
he didn't leave the table. Flo put the paper on the
sideboard and began clearing the table, removing the
plastic fruits in the cut glass bowl and the white plastic
doily. Efficiently, cheerlessly, they worked around him.

Suddenly, Flo jostled his elbow. He glared at her
suspiciously. She was looking up, past the living room,
squinting at the darkened foyer.

"Where ya been?" she called out.

Frank hadn't heard anything, any door open or
close, but sure enough, Tony walked out of the darkness into the living room. He was staring right at Flo,
but he didn't answer her.

"Your ma asked where ya been?" Frank said. He
waited a second but Tony just looked at them, from
Flo to him. "Where ya been!" Frank demanded.

"Hey, didn't your pa just ask you something?"

Tony stared at them as if they were TV charac-
ters he'd discovered while randomly flipping chan-
nels. He blinked and tuned them out. Then he
turned, walked over to his grandmother's chair and
bent down to kiss her. "Hey, *bella*," he whispered. She

raised her cheek to receive his kiss and smiled contentedly.

Linda passed him. He tugged at her black hair playfully.

"Hey, Shrimp, how's it going?"

"Stop it," she squealed, "hi, ya."

"Dinner's late because they were out of a lot of things at the market," Flo hollered at him as he headed upstairs. "But, if it was normal, you would have been late."

Tony's bedroom was small, but it was all his and the door locked. It was just above the kitchen and next door to the bathroom. The house was old, the wiring vintage and, sometimes, when his mother used an electrical appliance downstairs, it slowed his 1000-watt blow dryer down. Tonight dinner was late. He hoped there'd be nothing to sap the juice.

It only took him five minutes to take his shower. Now, wearing only a pair of blue bikini briefs and his St. Christopher medal, he sat at the edge of his bed staring at the dryer. It was plugged in and resting on the ancient dresser that had belonged to some long-gone relative or other. No one in the house seemed to remember where it came from, just that it had "been in the family." Sometimes he tried to imagine who might have owned it. Mostly, he liked to think that it had belonged to someone who had escaped, who had suddenly, mysteriously, gotten too rich or restless, and vanished into a better life leaving his cast-offs to be picked over by the ones who stayed behind.

The dresser had been painted over many times. It was scarred and ugly, but it boasted a good-sized mirror attached to the top and framed by two gracefully curving pieces of wood. Bobby C. had once inspected the dresser. His guess was that there was oak under all that paint and that the wooden pieces to which the mirror was attached were probably hand-carved. Once they had even talked about maybe scraping it down and selling it. The mirror was indisputably a good one. Bevel-edged, old, and heavy

as hell. It was nothing like the new kind, the five and
dime fun house mirrors that made you over in their
image. His sister, Linda, had one of those in the room
she shared with Grandma. That freaky cheap mirror
was probably why the Shrimp was always complain-
ing about being too fat or too thin.

Tony stood up and approached the dresser. Head
lowered, he reached slowly, off-handedly, for the
blow dryer. He lifted it as if it were a loaded and
cocked gun. Holding it, weighing it in his palm, he
turned his back to the dresser. He closed his eyes,
counted to three slowly, then took a deep breath. He
filled his lungs as full as they would go and held the
breath. Without releasing the air, he whirled around.
The blow dryer was gripped hip high in his fist like
a gun, pointed at the mirror from which a man with
dripping wet hair and an enormous chest, a man
whose jaws were flexed and lips sealed and nostrils
flaring—a dangerous man, *hombre*—was staring back
at him.

He held the breath. He held it while he sprayed
himself with Brut and flicked the dryer on and blew
his hair almost dry and lifted his natural-bristle styl-
ing brush off the dresser and began to shape and
blow and perfect his hairstyle. His eyes narrowed with
the effort of holding the breath. His jaw muscles flexed
and his face grew dark. Still, he held. He walked to
his closet and opened the door and through his slitted
eyes almost couldn't focus on the meticulously ordered clothes inside.

Finally, he bowed his head before the fourteen
floral shirts, five suits, eight pairs of shoes and three
leather jackets that he owned and allowed his lungs
to empty with a whoosh. He raised his head slowly.
He held on to the knob of the closet door. He let
his cleared gaze move deliberately across the brilliant
array of clothing before him. As always, the sight
brought a special surge of energy and pride that
signaled the climax of his purification ritual.

He browsed without touching, remembering the

feel of each fabric, computing combinations of color, feel and fit. When, at last, he did reach out, he knew precisely which shirt, trousers, shoes and belt he would wear and whether he'd need one or two neck-chains, a gold horn or a cross or a medal, to perfect the outfit.

It took time to tuck his shirt in just right, to ad-just and smooth the hem so that his dark gabardine trousers fell flawlessly over the shirt tail, tight and right around his hips and ass. He was examining the folds of his trousers for the third and final time when his father came into the room.

"Hey, dinner's on the table. Come on."

"I ain't hungry," he said. He could feel the panic rising in him. It had taken an eternity to tuck his shirt just right. That wouldn't mean anything to them, though. "Honest," he tried again, "I ain't."

"Hey, just 'cause you're kicking in for the food, don't mean you don't have to eat it no more. You still got to eat."

Tony turned his back on his father. "It's a clean shirt," he said into the mirror. "I just put it on."

"So take it off," Frank told him.

"I got it on just right."

He could see his father's reflection in the mirror. "Hey," Frank said, irritation starting to creep into his face and voice, "you got nothing to be afraid of. Your mother's spaghetti sauce don't drip. It don't taste and it don't drip." It was a funny line, but Frank Manero wasn't smiling. He didn't smile. What he said was what he meant and he didn't consider himself a joker.

"Come on, hey. We're eating." The conversation was over. His father left the room.

"Fungule," Tony bent his arm and threw a fist against his bicep. He checked himself out one more time in the mirror. He adjusted his medal so the chain clasp was centered at the nape of his neck, then he followed his father out of the room and downstairs.

They'd already begun eating, except for his grandmother. She was rummaging in the dining room closet where his mother kept the holiday tablecloths, clean dish towels, and extra linen.

"Mama, come eat," Flo urged her.

"*Espetta!*" the old lady called impatiently. Then she came to the table carrying a folded white bed-sheet. She walked over to Tony. Standing behind his chair, she opened the bedsheet and draped it around him like a barber protecting a favorite customer's shirt. "*Mange buone,*" she said. She patted his head and, instinctively, he ducked, then furtively re-arranged his hair as she returned to her seat.

Frank looked sullen. "Bad enough you gotta be late," he grumbled, "you don't gotta make her wait, too."

"I can't leave work early to make it in time for dinner. You know that."

"You should have been a priest like your brother. Then you wouldn't have to worry about a job," Flo said solemnly and she crossed herself.

Tony's anger flared suddenly. "Everytime you mention Frank Jr., you gotta cross yourself?"

"He's a priest, ain't he?" she said defensively. "Father Frank Jr., your brother." And she crossed herself again, but swiftly this time.

Tony wanted to gag on his spaghetti. He felt his father's eyes on him. "Hey, your ma, she ain't got a lot to cross herself about," Frank said.

"Jeez, Tony. You're so jealous of Frank Jr." This time it was Linda sticking in her two cents. His impulse and rage were too quick to control. His hand shot out and he shoved her shoulder. She shrieked indignantly and, like a chain reaction at incredible speed, Frank slapped Tony and Flo reached out and pushed Frank. That was where it stopped but only long enough for Flo to realize what she'd done and gasp. Frank appeared stunned. He stared, unbeliev-ing, at his wife then slapped her soundly. Almost at once, they turned away from one another and Flo slapped Linda and Frank hit Tony again.

"*Basta,*" the old lady commanded. Except for a

final whimper from Linda, they all fell silent and resumed eating.

"I . . . I got some more pork chops, more spaghetti," Flo offered.

Frank didn't look up from his plate. Between mouthfuls, he said, "Where the hell you got more pork chops? I'm out of work."

"Long as we got a dollar left, we eat good in this house. I might even get a job. Maude says . . ."

She never finished the sentence.

"Like hell you will!" Frank roared. He threw his fork down and glared at her so hard that the veins on his forehead stood out and you could almost measure his blood pressure by their pulse. "Twenty-five years I been bringing home a good paycheck every week, busting my back. Then I get laid off—seven months, eight months—all of a sudden you're talking back. You're hitting me. *Talking about a job and hitting me!*"

Flo toyed with her spaghetti miserably. "No hitting," she said, meekly. "No slapping at the dinner table—that's the rule. And you were hitting."

Frank knew things were changing, little things, attitudes. Now, it had been confirmed. He looked wounded, a bit dazed. "You never hit me before, never," he accused. "And in front of the kids."

They ate silently for awhile. All of them were aware that a momentous event had just been acted out at the table; that they had witnessed—and worse, participated in—something crucial. No one wanted to acknowledge the event, however. No one really wanted to know, with certainty, just what had happened or consider what the personal consequences might be.

Tony, protected by the bedsheet, devoured his food. He didn't taste it; he hardly even chewed it. He ate huge amounts quickly and indifferently. His movements were constant and mindless. He twirled spaghetti onto his fork, shoveled it into his mouth and, before the last dangling strands had been sucked through his lips, his left hand was already reaching for the bread and his right aiming the emptied fork at a pork chop.

Finally, Frank pushed his plate away. He turned to Tony. At first, his voice was disturbingly subdued, almost apologetic, but it grew stronger, more assertive, as he reclaimed his patriarchal authority.

"I was going to get you into the union, but there's no work. Ya understand? I mean if there was work like it was before, you'd be in there. I'd have got you in already and you'd be working union now. Hey, you listening? You understand what I'm telling you?"

Tony had heard it all before. He didn't look up. "Sure. Yeah, pa," he said.

"No. No, goddamn it! You don't understand that. You don't understand nothing."

"What's to understand?" Tony asked.

Deliberately this time, but fast, Frank smacked him then turned to Flo and glared at her defiantly. She wanted no part of the challenge. In her own way, she was grateful that he had set things right again. She had her duties and responsibilities; he had his.

"Tony," she said, "you want to walk me to church?"

"Didn't you go already?" he asked her. The slap was forgotten. It hadn't hurt anyway and if he counted every time either of them reached out to whack him he'd have passed infinity a long time ago. He didn't forgive his father. The fact was he would have felt completely out of line even presuming to forgive him. A slap from your old man was a slap from your old man. It didn't need or ask for forgiveness.

"I went for confession," his mother said. "Now I want to go back. I got to . . . I got to pray for something."

"What?"

"For Father Frank Jr. to call me."

Tony groaned.

"Why don't you call him direct, Ma?" Linda asked.

"I want him to call me. A son's supposed to call his mother, not the other way around."

Tony shook his head, wonderingly. "You've gotta have God make Frank Jr. call you?"

"That's right," Flo said with authority and conviction.

"Hey, Ma," Tony told her, "you're turning God into a telephone operator, you know that?"

Nevertheless, after the women had cleared the table and left Linda to do the dishes, Tony put on his special studded leather jacket and escorted his mother and grandmother to the church. It was a cool night and they walked through the quiet streets quickly and silently. Flo had her arm tucked through Grandma's. The old lady clasped her rosary as if for warmth. Still, she looked more comfortable in her ancient black coat and hat than Flo seemed huddled inside the synthetic fur collar of her stylish new cloth coat. Flo seemed pensive. As they drew nearer to the church, she eyed Tony thoughtfully.

"You was always no trouble," she said suddenly. "I didn't have to worry about you, didn't have to give you no attention. You took care of yourself. A slap now and again, that's all you needed. You always got along nice by yourself."

She seemed to be thinking aloud and expecting no response so Tony didn't respond. But, was she telling him that Frank Jr. had been different, had needed more? Maybe. Maybe he was supposed to feel proud that all his mother thought he'd needed from her was a slap now and again. He did feel proud. He did take care of himself, always could, always had. So how come his brother was a saint and he was a shit?

Outside the church, he glanced indifferently at the statue of Christ. "Non-union," he murmured.

"*Che fa?*" his grandmother asked.

"Jesus was a non-union carpenter," he told her in

English and, when she appeared confused, he said, "*Niente*, Grandma," apologetically and let her stroke his face.

He watched them disappear into the church. He reached into his pocket for a cigarette, changed his mind and, taking a deep breath instead, raced wildly down the block and across the street to the corner where the Faces, rowdy, ready, dressed and pressed into Bobby C.'s Chevy, would be picking him up.

Joey was a little bull; built like one and, occasionally, as belligerent. He'd seen *Rocky* five times. He'd compared Sylvester Stallone's muscles one-for-one with his own four out of the five times and come away not feeling too bad. He loved that movie even though he thought Rocky came on a little too dumb, a little too soft, sometimes. Double J. thought Rocky was too soft, period. Especially when Rocky walked this dirty-mouthed little girl from the neighborhood home and practically let her shit all over him. No girl, little or big, could get away with talking like that to Double J. No guy, either, for that matter.

"There he is," Joey said to Bobby C. who was driving the old, red four-door Chevy.

Tony was waiting on the street corner. He was leaning up against a store window, slouching and smoking a Winchester. When he saw the red Chevy approaching, he tossed his cigarette away and ambled over to the curb. The car slowed, almost stopped, in front of him and he reached for the door.

"Floor it," Joey hissed to Bobby C. who hit the gas pedal, leaving Tony cursing furiously at the curb. As the car drew away, Joey looked back. Tony was shaking his hand, examining the index finger that had almost been caught in the door handle, and still cursing.

"Okay, enough," Double J. called from the back seat. He and Gus had been passing the vodka bottle back and forth. Suddenly he was miffed at not having been consulted on the action up front. "Pull up, you asshole," he ordered.

Bobby C. stopped the car. Bobby C. was slender and supple, usually over-quick in his movements. He tended to drop off into brooding reveries, then catch himself and tune into the group again with exaggerated animation. He'd been off in his private twilight zone when Joey had goaded him into hitting the gas pedal like that. Now, he looked into the rear view mirror and saw Tony under the street light.

"You dumb fuckhead," he grumbled at Joey.

Double J. leaned forward from the back seat. His torso wedged between Bobby C. and Joey, he extended his arm and began honking the horn repeatedly.

Joey stuck his head out the window. "Come on," he yelled at Tony. Then, to Bobby C.: "Stubborn fuck won't budge."

Bobby C. slammed the car into reverse. The impact knocked Joey's head soundly against the window frame. "Hey," he shouted aggrieved. Then he pulled his head inside like a turtle on speed as the Chevy rocketed backward, narrowly missing a moving car and jolting to a stop in front of Tony, who was still wiggling his injured finger.

Gus was cracking up in the back seat. Gus was almost always either wise-cracking or cracking up. "Shake that thing, disco king," he called to Tony. Then he howled like a dog and Double J. joined in, hooting and then they were all barking and whistling and cracking up until—with silence and dignity, with cool—Tony climbed into the back seat. As Bobby C. whipped the car into motion again, Tony said, very quietly, "You morons. You almost wrecked my favorite finger." And he held the finger up, revolving it slowly, to show them which one he meant.

"We got a couple of poppers," Double J. said. "Couple of poppers, three bennies, two joints and a half a fifth of vodka."

"That's all?" Tony said contemptuously.

"That's it. You want something now?"

"No," he said firmly. "And we ain't dropping anything till I say so."

"Aw, Tony," Bobby C. called from the front.

"Bullshit," said Joey.

"I mean it."

"Why the fuck why?" Gus demanded.

"I got my reasons," Tony told them.

It didn't matter whether he had or hadn't. His tone of voice was enough. It was the end of the discussion. The others acquiesced, lapsed into silence, sullen, at first, but compliant. The premature burst of rough-edged energy had been efficiently dissipated. They drove out toward 2001 Odyssey—not laid back, but held back. Bristling with expectations. Disciplined. Waiting.

The car moved through the night. They sat still, each holding his own space. They sat silent, recharging, conserving, contemplating the energy they had been willing to waste a few minutes earlier. It was a week's worth of energy bought at a high price, paid for in drudgery, duty, routine. Eight hours a day, six days a week, they paid. Tonight, they would spend— lavishly. But not yet.

Tonight, when they entered 2001, the world would reverse for them. All week long they were menials, wage slaves. Tonight they became The Boss. They owned the place—and it was *the* place, the only disco in Bay Ridge that really mattered. Tonight they were Faces. Everyone else existed to serve them—the bartenders, the bouncer, Bernie the DJ, the girls—all the girls. But not yet. They were still outside.

They drove past the familiar wasteland of auto shops, transmission specialists and alignment centers; past two-bit bar and grills blinking neon at the shadows of abandoned factory buildings. A small red light appeared ahead. Without visible or verbal communication, the energy level in the car picked up, began to crackle. Tony took a breath that emptied like a sigh. Double J. rubbed his hands together. Gus pulled the vodka bottle out of the seat corner. Bobby C. straightened up behind the wheel, shook his curly head once and re-entered Face space. Joey turned in the front seat and reviewed the trio in the rear. "Looking good," he said, then turned back around and focused, as they all had, on the red light that belonged to 2001 Odyssey.

Even as they pulled up in front of the disco, there was still time to prepare. They had an obligation here that was almost military. First reconnaissance: there were two lines out front, about fifty people in ragged formation moving restlessly in front of the disco door. That meant that the timing for their entrance was almost perfect. If there were fifty on the street, there'd be at least fifty more crowding around the ticket seller's table inside; maybe seventy-five tripled up at the bar. The dance floor would be crowded, but about half the dancers would be girls with girls. As for the couples. At least half of them would be total non-Faces, lames, zombies; people who wore the wrong clothes or made the wrong moves or were still working on last month's routines.

When they'd checked out the crowd in front of 2001, Bobby C. pulled the car up a little way and parked. They climbed out, then separated casually for uniform inspection. With minor variations, they were all dressed alike.

Joey fingered Double J.'s jacket, flipped it open for a look at the floral shirt underneath. "Okay, Double J. Looking sharp, tonight!"

"Dressed to score," Double J. said. "Horny, man. Horny. You know what I mean?"

"Know what you mean." Gus adjusted the gold-plated charm hanging from Joey's neck. Then he whirled around on his platforms and punched Double J. lightly on the arm. "Horn . . . eeee!"

"Hey, anybody scores gets ten minutes in the car, you understand?" Joey laid out a rule. "Ten minutes. Then you get out for the next guy."

"Make it in five," Double J. decided, "you get the Medal of Fucking Honor."

"Okay!" Tony said, calling the ego-hype ritual to a close. "We're the Faces around here. Remember!"

They remembered. They remembered that in all

the boroughs of New York, all over the country for
that matter, millions of kids went to school, went to
work, did their homework and went to sleep without
ever having really woken up. They were dull, dummies; so much the same that you couldn't, and
wouldn't even want to, recognize them. They were
anonymous. A vast anonymous herd of zombies from
coast to coast. Faceless.

Then there were the few, the chosen few, who
knew, instinctively, how to move; how to dress; what
the protocol was for every situation. They knew how
you behaved with your friends and how you acted
with everyone else. The dummies, you didn't even
see. The girls, you did the choosing and the using.
Parents, you showed respect. Enemies, you destroyed.

There were rules and qualifications. Inside them,
you were safe. You were safe and a Face in 2001 if
you were Italian and young and knew how to dance
and dress and curse and treat women with contempt
and sex casually. You had to have a basic wardrobe
of body shirts and the right jewelry, which meant a
couple of neck chains, a cross, medal, or macho charm
like a tiny twisted horn or gold "shark's tooth." You
had to look good, which meant tough. Play cool,
which meant tough. Be ready, always, when tested,
to win . . . which meant you had to be cool and
tough, always.

A squadron in loose formation, the Faces moved
out toward the discotheque. Their pace was brisk,
but not hurried. Tony was up front. His shoulders
swung with studied arrogance. Bobby C. had his hands
crammed into his pockets. His head was down. Joey,
walking beside him, nudged him surreptitiously and
Bobby C. raised his head, grateful for the reminder.
Gus was smiling. There was a feeling like a crazy
giggle in his throat but he kept the smile cool.

When they reached the front of the Disco, they
fell naturally into single file behind Tony. The crowd
at the door separated as they moved through.

"Hi ya, J.J." A girl, so heavily made up that it
was impossible to guess whether she was pretty or not,

only that she was young and trying too hard, reached out and touched Double J.'s sleeve as he walked by. Immediately, Double J. stopped. He faced the girl. His look said, "What are you, crazy?" Then he turned away from her and continued on. The girl fell back into the crowd, stung, chastened.

Inside, the red-on-red entryway was packed. The crowd in the ballroom was almost capacity and the mob around the ticket seller's table was frustrated, shifting restlessly, waiting for things to loosen up inside.

But the Faces procession moved, unchallenged. Through guarded glances of resentment and curiosity, they made their way to the ticket table.

"Hey, Tony." The girl behind the table beamed a welcome. Tony put the money for admission, the exact amount—six dollars, a five and a one—down on the table and held his hand out for the girl to stamp it. "Whaddya kiddin?" she laughed. "When'd I ever check your hand? Go on in." The others didn't bother to hold their hands out for the girl. They just laid their money down and followed Tony.

The room they entered consisted of a spacious dance floor now filled with bobbing, shaking, whirling young bodies, some doing variations of the Hustle, most involved in older, non-touching, disco dances. The music blared out of wall speakers; music as hyper and loud as Bernie, the disc jockey, himself. He was a wiry, non-stop dude in his late twenties. Up in his control booth, he tended to his records, turntables and amplifiers as lovingly as a lunatic gardener who'd been granted half an hour to weed a cow pasture.

The dance floor was backed by terraced levels of tables. Glittery materials and sheets of foil covered the walls, reflecting psychedelic bursts of color from the perpetual motion light machines. Spots revolved, spun, sprayed the air with multicolor beams, flashing randomly, on objects unexpectedly human.

The dance floor was packed. The terraced tables, from the topmost tier to the exclusive first level, were littered with glasses and overflowing ashtrays and liquid puddles and soggy cocktail napkins and sweating people—restless, restless. Only one table in the cavernous room was clean and empty. A black-and-white card in the center of it, authoritatively proclaimed it: Reserved.

The Faces made their way to the clean table in the middle of the first tier. Their table. Moving across the room, Tony nodded in greeting occasionally. He smiled his lop-sided half smile. He waved once or twice, although the gesture was so minimal, so vague, that any of half a dozen people in the area at which it was aimed might claim it as directed especially at them.

Three girls who had been sitting, fanning themselves with drink lists at a table two terraces above the Faces, became animated suddenly. Two of the three hurried off to the ladies' room to refresh their makeup. The third, stationed to guard the table, tried to check her face in the mirror of her blush-on compact and was vexed by the endlessly changing lights. She tossed the compact back into her purse. She rested her chin in her hands. That way, she was prepared. She could lower her face or raise her hands for cover should any of the Faces turn and see her before her friends returned and she could get to a decent mirror.

The Faces arranged themselves at the Reserved table. Double J., Gus and Joey scanned the dance floor aimlessly. Tony surveyed the tables with studied nonchalance. He wasn't ready to look at the dancers yet. Bobby C. pulled a small pad of paper out of his jacket pocket and set it down on the table. A waitress passed. He hailed her and, although they weren't sitting in her section, she asked him what he wanted. When it turned out to be a pencil, she gave him hers and hurried off to get another for herself while he began sketching. His eyes darted from the pad to the dance floor and back.

Finally, eyes fixed firmly on the pad, he asked, "Is Pauline here? Anybody seen her?"

"No," Double J. answered.

"Ain't seen her."

"No."

"Good," said Bobby C. He flipped a page of his sketch pad and started a new, looser drawing.

A blonde waitress, in her mid-twenties and, therefore, beyond their interest range, came by to take their order. They had appraised her once, as she approached the table. After that, they didn't bother to look at her again. They announced their choices like a squadron sounding off: scotch and soda for Double J. and Gus; vodka and tonic for Joey and Bobby C.; seven and seven for Tony. They felt her leave.

"Who wants to see the Knicks Tuesday?" Gus asked.

Tony turned on him sharply. "What the hell you talking about the Knicks now!?"

"Here comes the president of your fan club," Gus said loudly, relieved that another topic, in the form of a plump but pretty little blonde, had presented itself quickly.

"Tony?" The girl was about eighteen and no amount of mascara, shadow or heavily penciled eyeliner could make her look older. Aside from her eyes, which seemed to be sagging under the weight of the cosmetics, she was cute. Her nose turned up at the tip, her lips were small and pouty. She was a little girl, except for her bust, which was abundant, and her voice, which ran a limited gamut between hot and hostile.

"Hey, Annette," Gus said, "You mind sailing those blimps out of my way. One minute I'm looking at the dance floor, then you turn sideways and everything goes black."

She ignored him. Her eyes were fixed on Tony. She called his name again, with the same questioning inflection in her voice, only she had dropped the tone to husky.

"Yeah," Tony said in a bored way and slowly stood up.

"Whaddya mean . . . yeah?" Annette demanded.

"I mean, yeah, I'll dance with you. But you are definitely not my dream girl."

He left her standing there and walked directly to the dance floor. By the time he had chosen his spot and turned, she was right where she was supposed to be with her arms slightly raised and held out to him, ready. Her face was just right, too—petulant. He knew it was because he'd hurt her feelings with that line, but she looked better when she was pouting. She looked tougher, sexier, than when she was all dripping with love.

"You want a dream girl, go to sleep and have a nightmare," she said meanly. And then her face softened and the hurt came through the anger. "You know, when a person likes another person a lot, you'd think the other person could like the person back a little."

He looked down at her. It was okay only because she was a girl and you couldn't expect a girl to understand self-respect, or the importance of being cool no matter how she felt inside. Still, he felt cheated that she had gone soft on him.

"Let's dance," he said.

She redeemed herself on the floor. She followed his lead flawlessly. She never missed a turn or messed up an intricate movement. He held himself tall, never looking at her, trusting his arms to inform her entire body about what the next move would be.

Up in the booth, Bernie was speed-rapping over the music, ". . . just remember—the way I sequence the records can take you zombies up or take you zombies down. . . ."

Tony and Annette never heard him. Bernie wasn't talking to them. He was talking to the jerk-offs. No one could take Tony down, not when he was dancing. No one could take Annette down when she was Tony's partner. Urged on by the music and their impeccable performance, Tony began to improvise. His inventions grew bolder, more savage.

Annette followed blindly, but not so blindly that she didn't see the girls on the dance floor watching or feel how space just opened up for them. No one stopped dancing to watch and no one, consciously, moved out of their way, but it was as if they were

glowing . . . putting out a radiance that drew people's
eyes toward them and kept their bodies away. Tony
led her into a final, dazzling series of spins and
whirls, executed at breathtaking speed. She was
flushed and slightly dizzy when he let go of her hand
and left the floor.

On his way back to the table, Tony stopped and
stared. He was hardly aware that he had. He only felt
his face muscles tighten and something jubilant go
out of him. Then he realized that he had stopped.
Angrily, he tore his eyes away from the black dude
who was dancing with a white girl. He didn't want
to let go of the high yet, so he filed away the image
that had angered and stopped him in his tracks.

It wasn't a common sight. Black on the streets,
okay, once in awhile. Everyone said the neighborhood
was changing. Black at a disco, okay, once in a while.
They usually came with their own, stuck with their
own, got frozen out and left fast enough. Black and
white guys mixing, okay, once in awhile—for a basketball game, maybe—or co-starring in a war movie.
But a black guy with a white chick—not in this
neighborhood, not in this disco, not in this movie, man.

Later for the black bastard, he decided. *Hombre, you will die.* He walked quickly back to the
Faces' table.

"You're the king out there, Tony," Bobby C. was
saying.

Tony rumpled Bobby C.'s curly hair. "Shit, you
practiced, you could dance as good as me."

Annette had trailed him to the table. Now she
stood beaming at him, an expectant look on her face.
She had kept up with him on the dance floor. She
was waiting for her reward—an invitation to join him.

"You really think so? You think I could dance
like you?" Bobby C. asked.

"No," Tony said.

"Ain't you going to ask me to sit down?"

Tony looked up at Annette as if he hadn't known
she was waiting there. "Why would I do that?" he
said. "If I asked you to sit down, you'd do it."

"But you'd ask me to lay down, wouldn't you?" she shot back at him.

"No. You wouldn't do it."

"Eff," she said petulantly, and stormed off.

"Hey, we're doing the speed now," Bobby C. told him.

"What the fuck's wrong with you guys?" he said. "How come you can't get off dancing?"

"How come you can, with spades humping white girls right next to you?" Double J. challenged.

Joey leaned forward. "Tony, what're we gonna do about that black dude?"

He'd already decided. "This time, nothing," he said. "If he shows up again, we'll put it to him."

"Hey," Gus called out indignantly. "Tony, hey, that guy's copying the step you were doing."

Tony took a long sip of his seven and seven. "Yeah, I saw that," he said without looking at the dance floor.

"Tony, can I wipe off your forehead?"

He and Gus looked up simultaneously. A chunky dark-haired girl was staring down at him. Her lips were actually quivering. She was holding her hands together over her heart, which was buried under layers of nondescript flesh, breasts that blended into belly. She was squeezing her hands together and they still shook.

Gus turned his chair around and buried his head in his hands. His shoulders heaved with laughter. "Mother of God," he wheezed.

Joey slapped Gus on the back. "Naw, it's only Doreen."

Tony touched his forehead. It was sweaty. He ignored Gus and Joey. There was a faint smile on his lips as he shrugged his consent.

Doreen pulled a clean white handkerchief out from under the cuff of her long-sleeved blouse and, tenderly, carefully, began to wipe the perspiration from Tony's forehead.

"It ain't no blow job," Joey sneered.

Double J. knocked down his second scotch. "You

don't know shit about women," he told Joey. "You get a blow job a hell of a lot easier than you get that."

"Oh, I love to watch you dance," Doreen was crooning. She blotted Tony's cheeks with the lace edged hankie. "I love it . . . watching you, you know . . . dancing. I love to watch you. The way you move and all, dance . . . I love to watch you dance. I love, love, love, love to watch . . . Tony, you know, you don't know . . . you don't know how I love to watch you dance and all."

"Hey, Doreen," Joey said. "Let me ask you something. You like to watch him dance?"

Gus almost fell off his chair. Double J. choked on an ice cube and couldn't seem to make up his mind whether to laugh or die trying. Joey, his humped nose held high in the air, snorted like a pig. Bobby C. looked up from his sketch pad. "She's a sweat freak. She just wants to wipe. She don't like dancing with him."

Even Tony's eyes creased with suppressed laughter. If he sat there for another minute with Doreen mopping his face, he'd crack. "Come on," he said while he could still keep a straight face. He grabbed her wrist, and dragged her after him to the dance floor. Half a second into the number, and he knew his chivalry was going to cost him, Doreen was as clumsy as she looked. She followed his lead badly, whimpering, "I'm sorry" at every misstep. Her apologies were so frequent they practically set up a syncopation to the beat.

He looked around him. Joey and Double J. were up and dancing, too. Their partners were okay, moved all right, didn't falter the way Doreen kept doing. Still, competent partners or not, Joey and Double J. were not in his league. He led Doreen into a spin, praying that she'd stay with him this time. He was trying to maneuver to a less central position on the dance floor.

Abruptly the music changed to a complicated Brazilian rhythm. Tony half-danced, half-dragged Doreen over to the control booth.

"Hey, Dees. What are you trying to do, man? Nobody can dance to that shit," he shouted up to Bernie.

Bernie leaned across his mikes and amps. "Oh yeah," he called back. "Check it out. What are they doing over there, huh? Check it out."

Over there, a couple was moving superbly to the Latin-Rock beat. The man looked older than most of the kids in the place. He looked, in fact, like a man. He was probably in his thirties. He was definitely conservatively dressed. He was good, but not as dazzling or intense as his partner who was tall and graceful and totally aware of her skill and impact.

The girl had brown hair with golden highlights and the way she wore it—just simple, loose and flowing—framed her high cheekbones and dark eyes and did more for her face than a ton of makeup would have done. She was not dressed as conservatively as her partner. She was too conscious of her body, too sensual in her movements, for that. Her clothing represented a compromise between vanity and class.

She was looking at Tony. Her dancing was flashy and flawless and she didn't break step for an instant, but her eyes were on him. He looked away.

His hand tightened on Doreen's hand. He gripped her waist harder. With his hands and his eyes, he was alerting her, warning her. Then, with no further preparation, he led her through a smashing sequence . . . disciplined, graceful; each movement and turn dictated by the music but inventive and personal.

Doreen almost succeeded in keeping up with him. She'd have it for a minute or two, then blow it and he'd improvise an instant adjustment to cover her.

He whirled Doreen sharply, held her steady for the beat, and shot a glance to where the brunette and her partner had been. He had to know if she was still watching. She wasn't.

Back at the table, he asked the Faces if any of them had ever seen her before.

"Her who?"

"That one," he turned back to the dance floor and pointed her out.

"No," Double J. said. Then, "Yeah . . . maybe. Maybe a month ago."

No one else had seen her before.

"She can dance," Tony said. "She doesn't have the right partner, but she can dance."

"So ask her," Joey needled him.

"Screw you." Tony said.

"Which position you want?"

He finished his drink and sucked on the skinny straw listlessly. The girl was still dancing. She hadn't glanced at him again. He wrapped the straw around his finger, unwrapped it, and finally shot it toward the floor.

" 'S' matter?" Bobby C. asked, not looking up from his sketch pad.

"Nothing," Tony replied curtly. "That's the matter. There ain't nothing happening or nothing the matter. It's just fucking hot in here. I'm going over to the bar."

There was a topless dancer on the horseshoe-shaped bar. Her breasts were small and loose, and when she tried to get sexy by bending over, they hung down, quivering dismally. Her G-string crept up her ass, a sequined line separated the jiggling globes. When she turned her back and bent over real low and flashed her bottom, it got to him just a little, though. The G-string was too small. It cut right into her crotch and you could see everything there but the sequins because they were being swallowed up by her flesh. He took a seat at the bar and watched her and started getting horny. Then he checked out her legs, from the slightly flabby thighs down to the skinny ankles, and then he cracked up. The topless, sequined, crotch-flashing dancer was wearing Earth Shoes . . . big, clunky, tan, fat-soled Earth Shoes.

"What'll you have, Tony?" the bartender asked.

"Is that for real?"

"What, her?" The bartender turned indifferently toward the dancer. As he looked up at her, she did one of her backward bends and the sequins disappeared into her shaved genitals again. "How much more real you need?"

"You going to ask her to dance with you?" Annette had sidled up to the bar and slipped onto the barstool next to him.

"So what's it going to be—the usual?" the bartender asked. Tony nodded. The bartender turned to Annette. "And for you?"

"Seven and seven."

"Right. Two seven and sevens." The bartender moved away.

"Oh my God, I didn't know that's what you were drinking, too," Annette said, obviously delighted and trying to expand the coincidence into a cosmic event.

Tony stared at her for a second then turned back to the topless dancer in the freaky shoes.

"They're having another sweepstakes," Annette said soberly.

"So?"

"So, double the prize money this time. Five hundred dollars."

"So?"

"We won before."

He turned to her. His eyes searched her face and she became flustered and blushed and finally looked down at her hands.

"Okay," he said reluctantly. "But we'll have to practice."

"Oh my God!" She was all soft and beaming again. "We'll have to practice!"

Tony kept his voice low and dispassionate. "They've got people coming in from Gazebo, Revelation, Manhattan . . ."

"Oh yeah! Oh, I know, Tony. Oh my God, we'll have to practice!"

"Hey, that's 'practice,' Annette. You got it? Practice, rehearse, you know. It ain't social. It ain't dates."

"Why not?" She was still excited, but an edge of petulance was creeping in. "We had a date. We went out once."

"Once, yeah. And once was enough."

"Why, Tony? How come?"

"I'll tell you how come. All you talked about was your married sister, then your other married sister, then your third married sister. I got the idea all you're interested in is getting to be a married sister yourself."

Annette began to protest. But the bartender came over with their drinks and Joey rushed up to them right after that. He was followed by a girl in a short rabbit-skin jacket. She looked annoyed. Joey looked angry.

"Hey, Tony," he blurted out, "Double J.'s been in the car twenty minutes!"

"So what?"

"So I can't get the selfish prick out."

Tony nodded. Without another word to Annette, he left the bar; Joey and the annoyed girl trailing after him. Outside, heading for Bobby C.'s car, Joey caught up with him.

"You gonna score with Annette?"

"I don't know . . . maybe," Tony said. "I don't want to."

Joey looked at him skeptically.

"You make it with some of these chicks," Tony explained, "right away they think you ought to dance with them."

Down the street, Bobby C.'s car was rocking.

"What's he humping, an elephant?" Tony asked. He, Joey, and the girl in the little fur jacket peered into the rear window.

"Mary Anne Grasso," the girl identified the flesh heaving under Double J.

"You were close," Joey told Tony.

Tony rapped on the window glass. "Hey! Joey says you've been in there twenty minutes," he called to Double J.

Double J. lifted his head. It bobbed up and down as he replied. "Twenty-five in the car. Twenty in the chick."

"Ten minutes, that's the rule. Get out or we'll pull you out."

"It ain't me," Double J. argued, breathlessly. "It's her. She ain't finished yet."

"You crazy? Since when do you care?"

Suddenly the rocking car picked up momentum. Double J.'s head bounced up and down like the head of one of those fuzzy rear window toy dogs. There was a great foghorn moan from the backseat.

"Okay, okay, it's happening." Double J. called. "Be out in a minute."

"You believe that?" Joey shook his head in disgust. "A chick finishing under these kinds of conditions?"

"Mary Anne Grasso," the rabbit-skin girl said, as if that explained it all.

Tony returned to the ballroom alone. He moved through the bar and the table areas quickly. Out on the dance floor, he spotted the graceful brunette and her partner again. He walked to the middle of the floor. Two girls were dancing together, side by side, working out a routine. He stepped between them, echoed their moves for a beat, then began to improvise.

The girls fell into step with him. One of them looked up at him dreamily. She seemed familiar. She was the girl who'd recognized him on 86th Street, the long-haired one. He turned to his left. The other girl was her friend, the one who'd said, "Oh, I'm dying, Donna."

He stared straight ahead. A couple joined them. A boy and girl hooked onto Donna's side, then two more girls, then another couple on the left. They were all following his steps.

One, and Two, and Tap, and Turn. And Tap, and Turn, and Tap.

He twirled and thought he caught a glimpse of the brunette heading for the door. He didn't see the guy she'd been with, though, the older guy.

"You know who you remind me of?" Donna gazed up at him. "Al Pacino."

"Yeah," Tony said, "I know."

The brunette was gone.

II

Sunday

In the paved lot that passed for a playground,
Bobby C. and Double J. were tossing a basketball
around. There were two hoops and two handball back-
boards in the lot. Those, and the high chain link
fence surrounding the sterile asphalt, authenticated
the lot as a recreational facility.

It wasn't exactly a city planner's dream. Wedged
between two commercial buildings, it was what it
was; a place to kill time or—occasionally, when things
got rough—a place to kill. It was a stage, a backdrop.
Depending on the temperament of its players, it
could be deadly or dull. Today it was dull.

Double J. jumped for the hoop as Bobby C. took
a shot. The ball spun once around the rim and top-
pled lamely to the pavement.

Tony scooped it up on the bounce.

"Hey, where the hell you come from?" Double
J. growled. He hadn't seen Tony enter the playground. When a pair of hands reached into the game
unexpectedly, his adrenalin coursed for a fight. Now
he had to cool out and he was miffed.

"From heaven. I'm scouting for the Knicks."

Gus and Joey crossed the lot.

"Toss it," Joey called.

Tony threw the ball to him. Gus sprinted forward
and intercepted it. He leaped up, exuberantly, clutching the ball and landed hard against Joey's chest.
Joey shoved him forward.

"What are you, crazy?" Joey hollered. He brushed some imaginary dust from the sleeve of his leather jacket. "You nuts, you know that, Gus? Just watch it."

"You better watch it, man," Bobby C. laughed. "There's a scout here."

Joey and Gus both looked around automatically. "Clowns," Joey complained when he realized he'd been had.

"Where?" Gus asked, still searching the yard.

"Here," Tony said, pointing to himself with his thumbs.

"Yeah. He's a scout."

"A girl scout," said Joey.

"Hey, find me a girl, then," Gus said to Tony. "You a girl scout, find me one."

"I got one for you," Bobby C. offered. "Pauline." He threw the ball at the basket. It thudded against the backboard, then dropped through the hoop.

"That the way you do it with Pauline?" Tony laughed.

Bobby C. retrieved the ball and whammed it at Tony's gut.

"See what the Knicks gonna pay Frazier?" Gus asked.

"Yeah," Bobby C. said. "Ain't gonna make that much in our whole fucking life."

"Makes you think about joining the mob, don't it?" Joey shook his head with mock bitterness.

"They wouldn't let you in," said Double J.

"Me? Bullshit! I had an offer—turned it down."

"Hey, Godfather," Gus said to Tony, "you make him an offer he refused?"

"Didn't like the pension plan," Joey said. "And I wanted a guaranteed prepaid funeral."

Gus dribbled the ball around Bobby C. "Hey," he said, "there's a Bruce Lee picture at the Orpheum."

"I seen it four times," Bobby C. said.

"So what? I seen *Rocky* five. You ain't going to see it again?" Joey accused.

"Sure. But not today." Bobby C. walked over to Tony and turned his back on the rest of them.

"Hey," he said, confidentially, "you know what? Pauline called me at home."

"Big deal," Tony said.

"No, man." Bobby C. tried to clarify it. He was really disturbed. "I mean," he said, pronouncing each word carefully and slowly, "s h e c a l l e d m e a t h o m e."

Tony tossed his hands up in the air. "How come you can't ever handle a girl?"

"I mean . . . *she* called *me!*"

Tony shook his head. There was disbelief in the gaze he shot at Bobby C., disbelief that turned to stony contempt. "Hey," he hollered to the other, "come on, let's cut this shit. Do something."

"Dirty Mabel," Double J. suggested.

"Boys, boys," Joey said piously, "you wanna gangbang on Sunday?!"

They filed out of the playground in ragged formation, Tony in the lead, Bobby C., looking hangdog unhappy, trailing the rest.

The Sunday streets were quiet. A couple of men were washing their cars. Some little kids on bicycles were racing up and down the middle of the otherwise empty street. Three women, each pushing a baby carriage, had converged at a corner and stood talking animatedly. One by one, the boys stepped off the curb and around the women and carriages. Bobby C. stumbled.

Gus turned, "What happened?"

"I wasn't looking," Bobby C. said. His ankle hurt. He'd smacked it coming down the curb.

"You okay?"

"Sure," Bobby C. said miserably, glancing back at the baby carriages.

86th Street had a little more traffic. The luncheonette was open and serving late breakfasts, mostly to solitary men. There were a few strollers aimlessly window-shopping.

Tony stopped in front of Shirtown. "Hey," Double J. said, pointing out the blue-striped shirt. "Sharp, huh?"

"I got a deposit on it," Tony warned. He was scowling at Double J., but glad that he'd admired the shirt, too.

Two men in their early twenties came out of the luncheonette. They were giggling together.

Joey saw them first. "Know why you don't kill fags on Sunday?" he said loudly to the others.

Double J. spotted the men now. They'd turned hurriedly and were walking down the block, away from the boys.

"You kill fags on Sunday, they go straight to heaven," Double J. explained.

Instinctively, the Faces started off after the men. They drew close behind them at the corner and lined up, single file, behind the couple.

One of the young men turned his head to look at them. He stared over his shoulder for a moment. His eyes flashed defiantly but fear overcame his initial boldness and he turned away abruptly.

The Faces followed mimicking the effeminate gait of the men; exaggerating the long-necked, low-shouldered posture, the swaying hips, the quick dainty steps.

"Right," Joey kept up his loud dialogue with Double J. "We don't want no fags in heaven."

"Right. Faggots in heaven, who'd want to die?"

"Maybe God's a fag," Tony said.

The other Faces stopped to stare at him; stopped and spun around and looked at Tony, astonished at his blasphemy.

The two young men hurried away unnoticed, forgotten.

Tony's crooked smile kept the Faces off guard for a moment. Then, Double J. said: "What're you kidding or something? That ain't no kinda joke."

"What kinda shit is that?" Bobby C. said.

"Faggots are to hassle," Joey said, definitively.

"Look at you guys," Tony laughed. "I saw something—that woman's free-your-ass movement or something—they were claiming that God's a woman. A woman! Okay, so if they can say God's a woman

—the fags got their movement now—sooner or later some of them are gonna start saying God's a fag. Lookit the angels," he reasoned with them. "They were all men."

"No," Gus argued. "They weren't either men or women."

"See, that's what I mean."

"What the fuck's the matter with you, Tony?" Double J. shook his head. "And your brother, a priest and all."

"Why don't you cross yourself when you say that?" Tony flared. "Like my mother does. Aw shit. I'd just like to make 2001 tonight."

"Do it," Joey taunted him.

"You asshole! Twenty, thirty bucks. You got twenty, thirty bucks to blow two times a week?"

"Aw, come on, Tony." Joey gave him a playful punch. Tony responded quickly, in kind, and laid one on Double J. for good measure.

"You dumb fuck," Double J. threw a slightly heavier shot at Tony who spun out of his way. The shot landed on Gus' elbow.

"What am I supposed to be here, your sloppy seconds?" Gus returned the shot open-handed. Shoving, punching, feinting playfully, the Faces loosed their crackling energy on each other.

"Sisters," Bobby C. hissed.

"Dumb fuck, who you calling a sister?" Double J. shouted and drew back his fist.

Joey grabbed and held it firmly. "Nuns," he whispered to Double J.

Suddenly, the tangled bodies, flying feet and fists, separated into five distinguishable human forms that stood at respectful attention as two elderly nuns passed.

"Okay, okay," Tony shoved Double J. The nuns were almost out of sight. "What the hell you doing?"

Double J. was still standing straight and motionless. "I'm Patton, asshole. Couldn't you tell?"

"You say something about patting asshole?" Gus crooned.

They all cracked up and Joey, Bobby C. and Tony followed Double J. who was chasing Gus down 86th Street. Gus ducked into a used car lot and taunted Double J. by doing a hide-and-seek routine around the lot. Finally, when the others caught up, Gus strolled out from behind a Mercedes.

"I'll take one of these," he said like a grocery shopper.

"No you won't," Bobby C. said ruefully. "You ain't never going to have that one. You ain't never going to have that kind of money."

"That your favorite speech?" Joey yelled at him.

"Well, he ain't. Nobody here is!" Bobby C. insisted.

Double J. spat in the dirt next to the Mercedes. No one said anything. They drifted over to a new model four-door Cadillac.

"My boss got a Caddy like this," Joey said. "And a Jag. Jag XK420. Got the Jag after he forced his partner to sell out. Gave him a real screwing."

"It's a dog eat dog world, ain't it," Double J. said.

"A rat race," Bobby C. intoned solemnly.

"Eat or be eaten."

"Everybody's out for what they can get."

An hour later, they sat dejectedly in Bobby C.'s old red Chevy driving along Shore Road.

"It's true. They got it all locked up," Joey said.

"Ain't gonna give you a chance."

"It's every man for himself."

"I want out," Tony said suddenly.

"What?"

"I wanna get out of the car," he repeated.

His request seemed to confuse the others. Double J. looked at Gus as if trying to confirm that they'd both heard the same thing. Joey half-turned, glanced at Tony dazedly, and faced front again. Bobby C. watched him in the rear view mirror.

"You got shit in your ears!?" Tony yelled at Bobby C. "I said I wanna get out!"

Bobby C. maneuvered to a stop and Tony got out. They were staring at him, amazed.

"You didn't ever do that before," Gus said in an awed voice.

"You leaving us?" Bobby C. asked.

Tony turned to the strip of park that led to the water's edge. From where he was standing at the top of the slope, you could see Staten Island and the Verrazano Narrows Bridge arching over the water. He thrust his hands into his jacket pockets, lowered his head, and walked along the path that ran between the road and the park.

The red Chevy followed him, kept pace slowly. Both Joey, in the front seat, and Gus, in the back, had their heads hanging out the window on his side.

"Hey, come on, Tony."

"Where you going?"

"Come on, man. Hey, we'll go see the Bruce Lee."

Tony felt really strange. He felt as though he might cry and that thought was so crazy that it brought a rush of fury with it which he unleashed on them. "Buzz off, scumbags!" he screamed.

Breathing hard, trying to fill his lungs, which felt constricted and tight in his chest, he turned away from them. He took a few steps down into the park, turned one last time to say, "I'll see you later for shit's sake," and took off at a run down the slope toward the river.

He never cried. Never in his whole life. Freaks cried, faggots cried, not Faces.

Once, when he was little—real little, so small that his father's hand could cover his whole face and there'd still be hand left over—his father and mother were having a fight. His mother was sitting at the kitchen table crying. His father was yelling at her. He was so little, he remembered, that his eyes could hardly see over the table top. Anyway, it looked like his father was going to hit his mother so, without thinking, he'd run between them screaming, "No, papa, no!" and had raised his hand against his father. His father had caught that hand and squeezed it—with one of his huge, callused hands; with the other, his father had grabbed his face and lifted him right off the ground. He'd held him there, in midair, hanging by the face, and he kept squeezing the hand Tony had raised against him.

There were three fingers broken on that hand. And purple fingermarks on his cheeks for a week. He hadn't cried.

He wouldn't cry now. He threw his arms back and opened his mouth to the wind and ran along the river's edge as fast as he could go.

Monday, he still felt like shit. Whenever there was a break at work, his mind would drift off. He kept thinking about Bobby C. and how they'd been friends, best friends, since first grade, since before that, even. But Bobby C. had gotten to him yesterday with his down rap about money. Bobby C., and all of them, going on and on about what a shitassed world it was and how you didn't stand a chance in it.

What had gotten to him, he had to admit, was that he half-believed it, himself. He was eighteen years old, almost eighteen and a half. Soon he'd be nineteen, twenty. What did he have besides Saturday night? Besides dancing? What in his whole life ever equaled that rush? That high?

Sometimes—lately, even at 2001—he'd look around the floor and realize that there was nobody over twenty-five in the place . . . and his lungs would get small just like they'd gotten in the car yesterday . . . nobody over twenty-five who mattered. Except, the other night, there was that guy dancing with the golden brunette. And he wasn't anything except her partner.

He'd been thinking about her, too. Would she have even looked at him if he hadn't been the best? So, the best what—dancer? Yeah. The best. It still meant something. The fucking disco dancing king!

"Beautiful. The stuff goes on beautiful, Tony."

He looked up. Becker, the house painter, was standing in front of him in splattered overalls and his white working hat.

"Hey, Mr. Becker," he smiled at the old man.

"Best vinyl paint I ever seen at this price," Becker continued.

"Told you."

"Saved me a piece of change on this job, kid. You know paint, Tony. You ever want a job painting, you let me know. You break your back, but you'll make twice as much as you make here. Interested?"

"I don't know," Tony said. He felt spooked and silly, like the old man had been reading his mind about money or something. He laughed at himself. "I don't know, Mr. Becker."

"Don't be interested," Becker advised. "You make twice as much, but you break your back. Ain't that right, Fusco?"

Dan Fusco had been listening to the exchange. When the house painter left, Fusco said: "Don't leave today, without seeing me, Tony. Right?"

"Sure."

Fusco winked. "Right. Now go figure out what that lady wants. She brought in a dozen different sample chips. You think maybe she's looking for a paint-by-the-numbers set?"

At six o'clock, in the little utility room in the back of the store, Fusco unlocked the top drawer of his desk.

"Monday. Payday. Hey, Tony?"

Tony was changing jackets. "Yeah."

Fusco came around from behind the desk and handed Tony his pay envelope. "I gave you a raise," he announced.

"A raise?!" Tony was surprised, delighted. He shoved the envelope into his back pocket.

"Ain't you going to look and see how much?"

"Nah. Gee, thanks, Mr. Fusco. A raise!"

Fusco lowered his eyes to the floor. "You better look," he suggested nervously.

"It don't make no difference. I never expected it."

"It's only two-fifty," Fusco confessed apologetically.

"So what."

"That's two dollars fifty cents. It ain't much."

"It's a raise.

"Tell you what," Fusco said uncomfortably, "I'll make it three-fifty. Next week it'll be three-fifty. A dollar more."

"You don't have to, Mr. Fusco."

"Shut up, will you. Four, I'll make it an even four." He turned his back on Tony and took off his jacket and loosened his tie. "Never seen anybody so shitass happy over a crummy two-fifty a week raise," he grumbled.

Tony bounded out of the back door of Bayside Paints and ran along the alleyway. He made a right turn instead of a left and found himself running back toward 86th instead of home.

The stereo shop where Bobby C. worked was open late Monday nights. Tony peered through the window of the shop. The record section was all lit up and active. It was separated from the rest of the store by a railing and a turnstile. There was a cashier's counter next to the turnstile. You couldn't get into or out of the record section without passing the counter and, if you were carrying anything big enough to smuggle a record in, you had to check it with the cashier.

Tony went inside. Tonight, a pimply kid named Paulie, the owner's nephew, was on duty at the counter. The rest of the store was quiet.

"Hey, Paulie, Bobby C. here?"

"Naw." Paulie looked up. Surprised and pleased that Tony Manero remembered his name, he smiled broadly.

"Oh yeah? How come?"

"Cause he's in stereo, the repair part, you know. They close down at five, no matter. Only the records stay open on Mondays."

"Do a good business," Tony remarked. It sounded funny, like he was a regular businessman all of a sudden. He grinned at Paulie. "Hey, I'll see ya, okay."

"Tony, Tony. Hey, come here, man!" The request

started as an urgent whisper but ended up sounding like a command.

Tony admonished him with a scowl, but the kid was already blushing and shrinking at his mistake.

"Please." Paulie amended his audacity.

Tony walked over to the cashier's counter slowly.

"Here," Paulie said, pulling an album from under the counter and thrusting it into a store bag. "I thought about you when it come in, so help me. I thought maybe I'd take it home and practice with it, you know. But I couldn't never do it like you, anyways. It's brand new and got two singles on the disco charts already." He handed the bag to Tony. "I'll tell Bobby C. you was looking for him."

Tony took the bag. Paulie was a weird kid. He couldn't dance, couldn't dress, his face always looked like a run-in with the killer bees. "Thanks," Tony said.

Paulie blushed again.

The kid is practically out of control, Tony thought. He couldn't help smiling anyway. A raise in his pocket, a record under his arm. Unbe-fuckin-lievable. Now, if only Bobby C. had been around. That was the point of his stop at the stereo store—to tell Bobby C., to show him, that it wasn't all so goddamned one-way gray like he saw it.

He ran all the way home. He ran inside, slamming the front door behind him, and raced upstairs to his room.

"You're late!" Flo called after him.

He tossed the album and his jacket onto the bed, then took the pay envelope out of his back pocket. He unfolded it. He smoothed it flat and set it down unopened on the dresser.

"You get down here or I'll feed your fuckin' dinner to the garbage pail!" his father roared. "This is still a family, you hear me. In this house you show respect!"

Tony picked up the hair dryer. He aimed it at the mirror, then turned slowly. Knees slightly bent, left hand resting low, careless against his thigh, he leveled the nozzle of the blow dryer at his bedroom door. "Your days are numbered, old man," he said almost silently, ominously. "You were the best shot around here in your day."

He straightened abruptly, set the dryer down on top of the pay envelope and went downstairs.

They were all at the table. He circled the table once—to kiss his grandmother's cheek and tug Linda's hair affectionately. Then he sat down and began piling food onto his plate. He didn't look up again until he'd finished eating. Grandma, Linda and his mother were clearing the table. Impulsively, he picked up his plate, silverware and glass and started toward the kitchen with them.

"What the hell you doing?" Frank hollered, shocked, outraged.

Tony stood still. He looked down at the plate in his hand then back at his father. "I don't know . . . just felt like it, that's all."

"Your mother does that. You don't do that. Your mother, the girls, that's their job."

"Hey, Pa, I got a raise," Tony said cautiously. "Old man Fusco gave me a raise."

"Whyn't you say so when we was eating?" Frank asked. His tone was still harsh, still abrupt but he hooked an arm over the back of his chair and regarded Tony with some surprise. "Everybody sitting around like a bunch of mummies. We could have used some conversation, some news. So how much he give you?"

"It's going to be four dollars. Was two-fifty today but then he raised it."

"Fusco, he raised your raise?"

"Yeah, when I didn't act disappointed with the two-fifty, he made it four, starting next week."

"Four dollars, shit!" Frank turned back to the table, turned his back on Tony. "You know what four dollars buys today. It don't even buy you three dollars."

The glass started rattling on the plate Tony was holding. He grabbed the glass and held it in his other hand, in his fist, as if it were a hand grenade.

"Oh yeah! I don't see anybody giving you a raise down at unemployment."

"Four dollars!" his father snorted in disgust.

Tony slammed the dish back onto the table. He was still gripping the glass. "I knew, yeah, I knew you'd knock it, piss all over it. Goddamnit, a raise says like, like you're good. You understand. You know how many times in my life anybody said I was good. Two fucking times in my whole life. This, the fucking raise and dancing at the disco. You sure as fuck never did!" He lifted the glass suddenly. His father drew back, stunned. He brought the glass down hard against the dining room table—not hard enough to shatter the glass, but enough to make the remaining dishes on the table jump and the salt shaker fall over. Then he stalked out.

Upstairs, after he'd showered and changed and was putting the finishing touches on his hair, his mother came into his room. She looked at him then looked away and started tidying and touching things.

"Ya got a raise. It's nice," she murmured.

"Yeah," Tony said.

She didn't say anything else so, finally, he turned back to the mirror.

Behind him he saw her looking at his posters, at the record album on his bed, and the briefs and undershirt and socks he'd worn and left laying there. She picked up the clothes and wandered to the chest in the corner. The top of it was arrayed with souvenirs and photographs, mostly snapshots. There was one of her and his grandmother standing outside the house. That one was in a plastic frame. The others were just lying there, piled loosely, one or two propped up against the plaster Virgin Mary on the chest.

She browsed through the snapshots. She stopped twice to cross herself and he remembered that he had some photos Frank Jr. had sent to him from the seminary.

"God get the message to him?" he asked his mother.

She shrugged, tired. "You look nice," she said and left the room.

Annette was waiting for him in front of Phillips Dance Studios. She was all huddled inside a fluffy fake fur. Her frosted blonde hair looked white in the street light. Her eyes were black with makeup and her little pouty lips looked black, too. When he got closer, he saw that they were glossed purple.

"You don't like the lipstick," she accused.

"That what it is?" he said. "I thought you just blew the Globetrotters. What are you doing down here. Why didn't you wait upstairs?"

She pulled a crumpled tissue out of her purse and began wiping the lipstick off. "I wanted to watch you come down the street, that's why. I like the way you walk."

"Shit," Tony said. He opened the door and went in. Annette rushed after him. Her heels sounded like a troop of tap-dancing mice on the stairs.

"I began thinking," she said breathlessly. "Maybe I'll make it with you."

He didn't turn around. "That's what you call thinking?"

She whimpered sullenly.

"Jesus!" he said. "You decide we're going to do it, so we're going to do it. That's it, huh? I got no say!"

"That time we went out you said you wanted to do it," she reminded him sharply. "You told me how horny a guy gets when he's eighteen. You told me how his . . . you know . . . how they ache if he don't get it. How they ache morning, noon and night . . . six days a week, sometimes seven, if he don't get to do it."

He stopped midway up the stairs and faced her.

"Annette," he said patiently, "we're going to be seeing a lot of each other practicing, rehearsing. If we was balling, too, it'd start to be like we were going together, you understand. And I don't want to be going together with you."

She looked hurt. But she snuffled once, then

tossed her head arrogantly and looked down the steps, away from him.

He kept on walking.

"Anyway, what are you," he demanded, "a nice girl or a cunt?"

"I don't know. Maybe both."

"You can't be both," he said definitively. "That's something a girl's got to decide. You've got to decide whether you're going to be a nice girl or a cunt."

He waited for her at the landing. "You understand all that?" he asked before they entered the studio. She looked up at him from under her mascara-beaded eyelashes and nodded like a spanked child.

Inside, Pete—slim and a little slimy, looking like a gangster's sidekick in one of those late night TV movies—was giving a class in ballroom dancing. The songs were older than the students, and that made the music practically vintage.

Tony leaned against the wall waiting for the syrupy music to stop. Pete saw him in the mirror. "Hey," he called. He shoved the woman he was dancing with toward a balding, middle-aged man who was cowering in the corner. "Come on, Mr. Farelli," he coaxed, "give the girl a break. She's a terrific dancer. You're terrific, honey. Honest," he told the reluctant woman.

"Hey, kid." He shook Tony's hand warmly. Hands on his hips, head tilted rakishly, he surveyed Annette.

"Who's the lucky lady?"

"Got a studio?" Tony asked.

"Six is free," Pete said, still smiling at Annette.

"How you been, Pete?" Tony asked.

"Zingy. Steady at sixty-five per cent," Pete laughed. "Studio six. See you later, Tony."

"Yuch," Annette said, as they headed for the practice rooms in the back. "Who is that guy? How come you know him?"

"He's like the manager here. He's a teacher, but he practically runs the whole place," Tony said proudly. "I sent him a lot of customers. People ask me. He gives me free practice time."

"What'd he mean by that sixty-five per cent?"

"He scores sixty-five per cent of the chicks who come in here."

"Sick," Annette said, wrinkling her nose squeamishly. "Hey, what's the matter?"

Tony had stopped suddenly and was staring into one of the practice rooms. He looked startled. Annette stood on her toes and peeked in over his shoulder.

A dancer, a girl in tights and a leotard was working out, alone, in the room. She was exercising to music. Neither the music nor the steps were terribly interesting. The girl wasn't much either, Annette decided. She had a nice figure if you like the type, which was a little too streamlined for Annette's taste, tall and willowy with no decorative curves worth mentioning. She had a decent bust, small hips, and a high but hardly outstanding ass. Her face was what you'd call attractive. You wouldn't call it pretty or beautiful or anything. Her skin was pale, her hair brown, mousy medium brown . . . natural, Annette noted with some distaste. Natural like in all those herbal, singing, clean and wholesome oatmeal-up-your-ass TV ads.

The girl hadn't noticed them.

"Hey, Tony," Annette tugged at his sleeve. "We rehearsing tonight or what?"

He continued quickly on down the hall and she practically had to run to keep up with him.

"You know her?" she asked when they'd settled in Room Six.

"Seen her at 2001," he said. He turned the wall switch on and the room filled with music—old music. He moved the knob till he hit the disco channel.

"You ever seen her?" he asked. They were in the middle of a complicated turn so it was hard for Annette to buy the extreme casualness with which he'd asked the question.

"Whaddya want to know for?"

"Forget it," he said.

He didn't mention the girl again. He became totally absorbed in the dancing. He led her through a polished but basic series of steps and turns, once, twice, three times. She had it. He reached out to the control knob on the wall panel and turned the volume of the disco music louder.

"You ready now? You watching?" He executed a new, more exciting sequence, in front of the mirror, alone. Then he took her hand and waist, and guided her slowly through the steps.

She was good, alert. She followed the lead. She almost had it on the first run through. "Okay. Real time now," he said. And they went through the sequence faster. This time, she missed an involved step.

"No, again." Tony ordered. They did it again—perfectly. "Once more." They did it. "Again," Tony said. They repeated the sequence. "Again."

"Sweet Jesus, Tony. It's only dancing."

He stopped dead. He stared at her with disbelief, with contempt. "What'd you say?"

"I'm sorry, Tony."

"Only dancing? That what you said. *Only?*"

"Aw, come on, Tony. Don't get mad. I said I was sorry, didn't I?"

He paced the room like a jungle cat. Finally, he turned the music down and said, "All right, okay. We've done enough. I'll see you Wednesday."

"Tony?" she said in that hurt little girl's voice. "You walking home?"

"No! I'm going to talk to Pete. Maybe work on something."

She shrugged and tossed her head as though his anger had never touched her. Then she got her coat and, with one of her hot and haughty you'll-never-know-what-you're-missing looks, stalked out of the room.

Tony lit a cigarette and leaned against the practice bar on the wall opposite the mirrors. He studied himself listlessly, turned to check his profile, did a few steps and smoked about half the cigarette before he was ready.

He walked down the hall leisurely. He could see from three rooms away that the door to the brunette's studio was ajar. There was music drifting into the hallway. He couldn't be sure it was coming from her room. He took a deep breath and held it and very slowly kept on walking toward her door. He just sort of put one foot in front of the other, like in the kids' game, Giant Steps. You may take ten Tony's foot-sized steps, heel to toe, heel to toe.

His face was pink when he let out the air. His eyes were slightly misty. He felt just the tiniest bit high, just high enough to move with supercool grace.

He nudged the door with his toe. It swung open easily, soundlessly; any mechanical flaw or squeak that might have existed was covered by the music which was faster and louder now than the warm-up stuff that had been playing earlier. She was there. She was dancing. Occasionally, she bent over or dipped down or swung her leg too high, limbering her muscles in the middle of a well-choreographed series of dance steps. It bothered him, that she could break the flow like that. But when she danced, she was as good as he remembered.

He watched and waited at the door for a while, then he walked into the practice room.

"Hi," he said. It wasn't exactly a movie entrance, but he tried to keep his voice pitched softly enough not to startle her and loud enough so she'd hear him.

She glanced at him and nodded and, without even noticing the sincerity in his eyes, continued her dancing and exercising.

"You're good," he said perfecting the pitch, moving it into the cool observer range. "You're a good dancer."

She nodded again, curtly.

"I want to meet you," he said.

She stopped, but only for as long as it took her to say, "Look, would you mind going away?"

He was stunned.

"Don't be hurt but . . ."

"Hurt?" He cut into her words, tried to run over them. "What do you mean don't be hurt?"

". . . I just want to be by myself." She finished her sentence, not hearing him.

"I want to meet you," he repeated.

"I don't want to meet you."

She sounded like she looked; different, half-natural, half-trying too hard. Her voice was like the clothes she'd worn the other night; obviously selected, chosen to seem classy, tasteful, but with undercurrents of the street coming through, not street tough, but street wise and sexy.

He didn't know exactly who he was talking to, a neighborhood girl or a stranger.

"How come?" he asked. "How come you don't want to meet me now? I saw you at 2001. You saw me."

"So what?"

"You saw me looking at you. I saw you. You were watching, you were looking at me."

Quietly, more to herself than to him, he heard her say, "Look at a guy longer than a millionth of a second, they get delusions of grandeur."

She turned her back to him and began an elaborate series of exercises. Her body was incredibly supple, stretching easily into positions that sometimes seemed impossible. She ignored him utterly. She bent backward forming an inverted U. Her body became a bridge. Her head was upside down, facing him. Her pelvis was arched high, toward the mirror.

He was mesmerized. He was angry. He felt helpless and he hated the feeling.

"You know what you are?" he said, finally.

"I'll bet it begins with a C, Mister P.," she replied.

He had no comeback whatsoever. He just stood there and stared at her. Finally, he left the room.

He almost expected to find Annette waiting for him when he reached the street. She wasn't there, of course, and he wasn't sure whether he was glad or not. He walked toward the pizza parlor, thinking vaguely that maybe Bobby C. or some of the guys would be around.

There were a few people in the parlor, a few couples. They were mostly older than he. They were mostly tired and not talking much to one another. Probably, they'd just come from the movies and were grabbing a bite before heading home. He didn't know what made him think that. He didn't usually look at people and decide who they were and where they'd come from or where they were going.

That was it, he decided. These people, these tired, quiet, beat-looking couples, it didn't take spit to figure them out. It was as if every one of them was wearing a giant identification tag: Married. Coming from Nowhere. Going to Nowhere. Period.

The counterman raised his head. Tony held up two fingers. The counterman nodded and took two slices out of the oven.

"You seen Bobby C. tonight?" Tony asked.

"No," the counterman said. "Been like this all night. Real slow."

Tony piled the slices one on top of the other. "You got one more already hot?" he asked impassively.

"Sure," the counterman said. "Hungry tonight, huh?"

"I ain't hungry," Tony said, turning away from the empty-faced couples. "I'm fucking starving!"

He finished the triple decker in record time. Outside, he kicked the crumpled napkin forward for awhile, jostling it ahead of him from foot to foot like a soccer player.

There was a phone booth at the corner. He kicked the napkin over to it, reached into his pocket for a dime, and dialed Phillips Dance Studios. He needed to know her name.

Pete picked up on the fourth ring. "I was just about to close 'er down," he said. He sounded annoyed. "I got a date."

"Yeah, well, listen, hold on a minute would you? It's important. I gotta find out something."

Less than a minute later, he was on the street nudging the napkin again. Suddenly, he sent it through the sewer grating with one calculated kick and jumped onto the curb, arms raised in victory. Then he ran home.

There was a light on in the living room. He unlocked the front door and went inside cautiously. The house was silent, but the light was on. It was too late for anyone to be downstairs. Something was wrong.

He peered into the living room. His parents were sitting on the couch staring at him. Their faces were unreadable, blank.

"How come you're up so late?"

They looked strange. His mother's hands were resting in the lap of her flowered cotton housedress. Her hands looked funny, turned palms up, just laying there as if someone had arranged them. Her hair was in rollers as usual, but some of the rollers were hanging loosely, lop sided. His father sat rigidly. He was wearing an undershirt and pants and his hands were gripping his thighs. You could see the loose brown material of the trousers wrinkling and bunching under his thick fingers.

They didn't answer him. They didn't look as if they'd heard.

"What's happening around here? I come in and you've got no criticism of me."

His mother sighed heavily. There was no other response, so he left them sitting there and ran upstairs.

There was a light on in his room, too. He could see it shining under the door. He looked up and down the hallway for a moment. Nothing else seemed amiss, no noises, no other lights. He opened the door to his room and entered.

A priest was standing in front of his closet examining the clothes inside.

"What the fuck?" Tony said.

The priest turned. He looked embarrassed at

having been caught staring at the clothes. He was stocky and dark and slow-moving; his shoulders drooped slightly. He lifted his head and, seeing Tony, his pinched face opened visibly and he smiled.

"Frank!" Tony shouted. "Holy shit! Frank!"

"Hi, kid," his brother said.

They embraced warmly; Tony so flushed with excitement, he almost lifted Frank Jr., off the floor.

"Hey, take it easy! Take it easy," the priest laughed. "I'm not used to this much affection. Give me a little time to adjust."

"Aw, hey, you look great!" Tony said, backing off to look at him.

"No, I don't. You do," Frank Jr. said appraising his kid brother with honest joy and admiration.

"Ma and Pa . . . they didn't say anything. I saw them downstairs. They didn't even tell me you were here."

Frank Jr. bowed his head, embarrassed again. "They're recovering from the shock," he said somberly. "I'm leaving the Church, Tony. I'm leaving the priesthood."

"Jesus Christ!" Tony said. He sat down on his bed and stared, wide-eyed up at his brother. His mouth was suddenly as slack and useless as his parents' mouths had been. Now he understood why they'd looked so strange. He looked down and noticed that his own hands had fallen between his knees, palms upward, empty like his mother's.

"Can I borrow some clothes?" Frank Jr. asked softly. "Just until I can buy some. I don't want to wear the uniform." He removed his jacket as he spoke. Under it, he wore a white undershirt and an odd black vest to which his clerical collar was still attached.

"Sure. Sure," Tony said, still somewhat dazed. "When'd you get here?"

"Couple hours ago."

"You're really leaving the Church?" He felt slow, dulled; unable to accept the situation. "What did

Ma say?" he asked, as if that would somehow make it real.

"She said, 'Dear Lord, what am I going to tell Theresa and Marie?'"

"And Pa?"

"Ashamed. Both of them. *They're* ashamed!" Frank Jr. paused to reflect on the irony. "Are you? You ashamed of me, Tony?"

Tony shook his head, no. "Didn't they ask why?"

"No." Frank Jr. smiled. "I think they're afraid to. Like I might say—celibacy."

Tony started to say something, then stopped. Finally, he looked back up at his brother and, smiling with him, said, "Well, where you going to sleep? Your old room's like a storage dump."

"I thought here, maybe."

"Here? My room? Wow, sure," he said jubilantly. "Sure, that's cool, that's great!"

He stood up quickly and started tugging at the upper mattress, trying to yank it off the bed. He pulled the sheets, blankets and pillows off carelessly, tossing them into the air behind him. Finally, he wrestled the mattress to the floor.

Frank Jr. was laughing. There was a sheet draped over his shoulder and he was holding one of the pillows he'd caught in midair. The second pillow was hooked up over the closet door. Tony straightened up and looked at Frank. Then he began to laugh, too.

"You know what this feels like," Frank Jr. said. "It's like reliving a childhood we never had."

It must have been two A.M. Tony couldn't sleep. He heard his brother breathing slow and steady in the bed. He sat up on the mattress on the floor and stared at Frank Jr. He just sat there in the middle of the night, in the dark room, watching, listening to his brother sleeping. He hardly even noticed it when Frank Jr. stirred and woke.

"Tony? Can't you sleep?" Frank called softly.

"No," he said. "Listen, I've gotta know. Frank, why? How come you're doing this?"

"A lot of things," his brother said after awhile. "I'll try, okay." He put his arms behind his head and stared up at the ceiling. Tony waited.

"A young priest," Frank began tentatively. "For a young priest, the life can be very limited, boring, sick calls, trivial errands for the pastor—it doesn't match your ideal of serving God by serving man. It doesn't seem, doesn't feel, spiritual. Then you begin to think of the Church's political activism, intrusions, its positions on birth control, sex, freedom of expression. But, most important, one day you look at a statue of the Madonna and Child and it doesn't have that mystic glow around it. Or you look at a picture of the Crucifixion and all you see is a man dying on a cross—not God, not the incarnation of God, not the son of God. A man. And you know your faith, the rock-like edifice of your faith, has more than a small fissure."

Frank Jr. fell silent and Tony was glad his brother had been staring up at the ceiling and not down at him. He felt uncomfortable—stupid, almost; almost scared. He had never heard Frank talk like that. He had never heard anyone say such things but, more importantly, say them that way, with such pain and love. It was like listening to the Pope. It made you feel proud, but kind of dumb; almost unworthy.

"You wonder," Frank Jr. continued softly, "were you ever really meant to be a priest. You're taught . . . they turn you into what they wish . . . at a time when you can't defend yourself against their fantasies—Ma and Pa with dreams of pious glory. And the nuns and priests spotting a serious, studious boy, their yearly candidate for the collar. Now I realize what I really believed in—*their* image of me as a priest."

Tony stood up and walked to the dresser. He couldn't just sit and listen anymore. He'd asked the question and gotten an answer that opened up more questions and it made him restless.

In the light from the street lamp, he saw Frank's shirt and clerical collar lying on the dresser. He picked the collar up and examined it curiously.

"Well," Frank Jr. said softly from the bed, "now that I'm the disgrace of the family, does it make you feel different? I'm not so perfect anymore, Tony. What about you? What does it mean to you?"

In the shadows, Tony shrugged. He turned the collar in his hands. "If you ain't so good, I ain't so bad," he whispered to the collar. "If you're not a saint, then maybe I'm not a shit." He carefully set the collar down on the dresser and laid back down on the mattress.

He liked the way the room looked in the morning. Frank was asleep, twisted up in a white sheet. The rest of the bed linen was on the floor. And, of course, there was Tony's mattress on the floor, too. And the room was a holy mess. Truly, Tony thought, looking at Frank's sleep-soft face, a holy one. It reminded him of how brothers shared a room on TV shows.

He picked out his clothes, and took them, with his Brut, brush and blow dryer, to the bathroom. He even considered foregoing the blow dry after his shower, lest the noise disturb Frank next door, but decided on a compromise. He towel-dried his hair briskly, brushed it, and then used the dryer—in the bathroom, where dampness could short it out or fuck it up someway—just for the finishing touches.

He climbed up on the rim of the tub to check out his full length image in the medicine chest mirror. From head to mid-thigh, which was as far as the meager mirror would go, he looked just fine. He'd have to be especially careful at the store today. Button the dust jacket up and stay off his knees no matter what rolled under an aisle.

He had decided yesterday that he wasn't coming home for dinner tonight. He had made his plan and Frank's return only reinforced it. For one thing, his parents wouldn't miss him or make a big fuss out of his not being there tonight. And, though he hated to desert Frank, he knew what they would try to do if he did stay. They would try to make him take sides with them against Frank, or against Frank's decision. He didn't want any part of it.

Suddenly, he remembered something Frank had said last night—that line about a childhood they'd never had together. He hadn't understood it last night. He still wasn't too sure about it. But, the way he felt waking up in that mess, seeing Frank, this morning; that TV brothers feeling—he thought that was probably what Frank meant, too. He wasn't going to let big Frank or Flo take that feeling away. Not tonight. He had other plans.

His father and mother were walking around like zombies downstairs. He tried to look properly somber, but it was difficult. He felt like shouting, like running. He felt terrific—and evil because something that hurt them so much was making him feel terrific. So he lowered his eyes and tried to look as serious and unhappy as they did.

"Don't say nothing to your sister or your grandma," his father warned as he passed them heading for the kitchen.

His mother crossed herself. "God get me through this day."

"Me, too," Tony added silently, "and fast."

He had a couple of hours to kill between the time Fusco closed the store and the time Pete said to be at the dance studio. He wondered whether Shirtown ever stayed open late. Probably not on Tuesday, he decided. He wished he'd remembered the shirt yesterday. But he hadn't gotten paid till closing and didn't know about the raise till then. Lunch hour today, he'd thought about nothing but Frank's return and tonight.

Now, he wiped the last bits of pizza sauce off his fingers and threw the napkin away. He was tempted to go back to the pizza parlor and get two more slices. It was dark out already. The street lights had gone on without his noticing. A couple of blocks up, there was a small grocery store; one of those mama-papa shops that had a little homemade deli counter. It was open. He could see the light and hear the little bell that tinkled every time someone opened or closed the door. Maybe he'd pick up some sliced ham and macaroni salad. Then head on over to Phillips Dance Studios.

As he crossed the street to the grocery store, Gus emerged carrying a full brown bag.

Tony fell into step beside him. "Hey, Gus, you shouldn't carry this shit," he said peering into the bag, "you're Gus the clown, Gus the joker."

"Only one first name on my birth certificate, man." Gus interrupted.

Tony wasn't listening. "You should juggle it all the way home," he said. He took two cans out of the bag and tossed and caught them. "Juggle everything in there—all the way home." He said juggling the cans.

Gus was grinning. He was annoyed at having been caught lugging a grocery bag home, and annoyed that Tony was ribbing him about it, but Tony's strange enthusiasm was contagious. Tony was grinning. Gus, resentfully, grinned too. Only his voice clung to his initial irritation: "Hey, what the hell's with you, Tony? You flipping out or what? Don't be callin' me a clown. And put those goddamn cans back before you drop one of them on my head. What the hell's with you?!"

"My brother Frank come home!" Tony twirled and caught the cans low down, too near the concrete for Gus' comfort.

"You're gonna bust one of them, you jerk-off."

"You hear me, Frank's home. He quit. My brother, Frank, he quit the church! He quit the church!"

"Hey," Gus said, awed. Then, still a victim of Tony's enthusiasm, he added, excitedly, "Hey, your big brother Frank, huh? Wow, that's great, Tony!"

"Yeah. He ain't going to be a priest no more! I feel kind of wild, you know? All this kind of energy!" He tossed one can very high up and caught it behind his back. Then he threw both cans back into the bag and ran off.

Gus watched him disappear down the street. Then, shrugging off Tony's craziness, he turned the corner for the long walk home. The grocery bag was filled to the goddamned brim and he could hardly see where he was going.

Tony hadn't realized it until he'd said it aloud to Gus. He was feeling wild, energetic. It was time to cool out, get it under control. At the dance studio, he forced himself to take the steps one at a time, though his inclination was to sprint upstairs.

In the main room, Pete was putting twelve ladies through a warm-up. The music was boring. The women were clearly neighborhood.

"She come in?" Tony called to him.

"I told you on the phone—she comes in on Tuesday."

"So she come in?"

"What day is it?" Pete sneered. Then, as Tony turned to open the door to the rehearsal rooms, he added, "Watch it, man. That one's practicing to be a bitch."

Tony held the door half open for a moment, shrugged and went on through. He walked slowly up the corridor pausing to peer into each small studio. She was not in the room she'd used the night before. He found her near the end of the hallway in a studio set up for gymnastics. She was alone again, practicing on the parallel bars. Her moves were as sure and graceful as he remembered, their impact as exciting as when she danced. He watched her quietly, enjoyed watching her; then braced but confident, he entered the room.

She seemed to be performing a routine. No movement seemed isolated from any other. Each flip and spin and reverse happened precisely where and when it ought. She seemed to be conducting the music with her body, not listening to it or straining for cues. He stood in the middle of the room watching. Finally she saw him. She glanced at him briefly and looked away without pausing or faltering in her gymnastic routine.

He didn't want to disturb her movements, but he wanted her attention. "Something I want to say," he announced. If she could see him and keep on going, she could talk the same way. For the moment, that was all right with him.

"You don't know a person, there's nothing to say to them, is there?" she said.

"If that's right, nobody would meet nobody, would they?" She didn't answer so he continued. "Your name's Stephanie. Your last name is Mangano."

He didn't expect it, but she stopped then. She said, "How do you know that?" With genuine surprise she slowed herself till she was sitting still on one of the bars.

He couldn't quite read her expression except that she was obviously surprised. He couldn't tell whether she was annoyed or flattered that he'd gone to the trouble of finding out her name. He thought she was pleased, thought he saw a momentary smile.

"My name's Tony Manero. We've got the same last initial."

"Now," she said with unmistakable sarcasm, "If we got married, I wouldn't have to change the monogram on my luggage."

"Someone said you were practicing to be a bitch," he told her. Immediately she looked stung and vulnerable. She tried to cover it quickly, but he'd hurt her . . . which, he realized suddenly, was not what he wanted to do.

"What is it you want to say to me?" she asked.

"Let's have coffee," he said.

"Was that it? That's what you've got to say?"

There was an awkward silence.

"You're a terrific dancer—not just good."

"I know," Stephanie said.

"I'm a terrific dancer. I wanted to say that, too."

"Obviously, you know."

"We could be a dynamite team. You and me, we could win the 2001 Sweepstakes, no sweat."

Pete had told him that she was neighborhood. It was hard for Tony to believe, but he was counting on it. She looked like she could have been an outsider. Most of the time, she sounded like one, too, except that her accent didn't quite know where it was coming from, just where it wanted to go. And she definitely danced Bay Ridge. Disco primo.

For the briefest instant, she looked interested. Then she was off and running again; running away from Bay Ridge.

"Dancing isn't everything," she insisted. "There's a world of difference between us—culturally, spiritually. It would get bigger, worse, every passing week."

"What kind of shit is that?" he said. "Listen, how about you telling me all about it—over coffee?"

They could have worked out a winning routine with all the time and concentration it took her to say, "Okay."

He waited downstairs while she changed. He didn't want Pete saying anything cute to him in front of her. Then he got nervous worrying about what Pete might say to her without him there. He smoked a whole Winchester and had just about decided to go back upstairs when she came out.

Simultaneously and without touching, they turned and walked together in the direction of the coffee shop. Her clothes were that same funny mix he'd noticed the first time he saw her—self-consciously conservative, but sexy. Under a beautifully tailored jacket, she was wearing light-colored pants and a sweater. The jacket's cut and cloth looked expensive, magazine-stylish. The pants and sweater looked expensive, too, but the emphasis of their fit was more on sex than style. On her head, at a rakish angle, she wore an outsized newsboy's cap.

"Where I work, the people are very remarkable

—so different from the people around here," she was saying.

"Snobs instead of slobs."

"What?" she said. He wasn't sure whether she'd heard or not. It was that kind of "What."

"This ain't the worst part of Brooklyn, you know. It's not exactly a hellhole," Tony said.

"It ain't," she said, ". . . isn't Manhattan. You have no idea how different, how it changes over there, just across the river."

Her whole voice had changed. She sounded as if she were describing a beautiful dream she'd had; as if she were dreaming it as she spoke:

"The people are beautiful, in Manhattan, the offices are beautiful, the secretaries, they all shop at Bonwit Teller. Even the lunch hours are beautiful. They let you take two hours if you do something related . . ."

"Related to what?"

"To work, to learning. We saw Zeffirelli's *Romeo and Juliet.*"

"Shakespeare wrote that," Tony said. "I read it in high school."

"Zeffirelli was the director. It was the movie . . . I mean, film."

"Romeo, he could have waited a minute," Tony said with sudden enthusiasm, "I mean, he didn't have to take that poison so fast. I . . . that always bothered me."

Stephanie looked up at him suspiciously. Then, in her other voice, the haughty, hard one, she defended Shakespeare, Zeffirelli and herself. "That's how they took poison in those days," she said.

Tony walked into the Venus II Coffee Shop ahead of her. The waitress seated them in a center booth, dropped two menus on the table, and left.

"You eating?" Tony asked.

"Just tea. With lemon," Stephanie said. "I . . . I started drinking tea recently. It's really more refined. The women executives at my office, they all drink tea. I . . . I've only been with the agency a while but I'm already operating in a public relations capacity as well as filling in for some of the agents. This week I had business lunches with Eric Clapton at Le Madrigal and at Cote Basque with Cat Stevens."

"Far out!" Tony said.

"You . . . you heard of them . . . those restaurants?"

"No."

"But you know who those artists are?" she asked nervously.

"No. Well, maybe sort of."

"Then why did you say 'far out?' "

"It sounded far out," he said. "Wasn't it?"

"Oh, Christ," she said and slumped back against the booth.

The waitress came over, pad in hand. "You decided?" she asked cheerfully.

Tony ordered: "Tea with lemon, three hamburgers and a coffee."

When the waitress left, Stephanie leaned forward again. "You know, Laurence Olivier was in the office the other day and he said . . ."

"Who's that?" Tony interrupted.

"You don't know who Laurence Olivier is?"

"No."

She didn't say, "Oh, Christ!" or fall back against the seat this time, but the message in her eyes was the same. Tony waited patiently for a reply. Finally, she said:

"He's only one of the most famous actors in the . . . oh, you know, the English actor who did the Polaroid commercials?"

"Oh, yeah."

"Well, he was in the office and I did a couple of errands for him and he told everybody I was really the brightest, most viv . . . viv . . . vivacious thing in the office in years."

"Could he get you one of those cameras, like at a discount, you know what I mean?"

"I didn't ask," she said icily.

"You already got one?" Tony asked.

The waitress delivered their order. She put the tea and one hamburger in front of Stephanie, the coffee and one hamburger in front of Tony, and left the third burger in the middle. She went to the service tray to get the mustard and ketchup. By the time she set the plastic containers down, all three plates were lined up in front of Tony. Only two burgers were left.

Stephanie stirred her tea daintily. "Are you enjoying what I'm telling you?" she asked unexpectedly.

"Sure," he said.

He hadn't really thought about it. He liked listening to her. He liked her wavering accent—the uncertainty, reflected in her voice, as she tried to leap from Bay Ridge to that other, more beautiful, more perfect, world across the river. What she was saying didn't matter too much. It didn't even matter that he suspected some of it was pure bullshit. He enjoyed her animation, the disdain she affected, the awe she couldn't conceal. It made everything she talked about seem vivid and important.

He remembered the couples in the pizza parlor last night. He couldn't imagine her among them.

"Why'd you ask?" he said.

"Because, well, maybe you can't handle hearing about a life so different than yours, you know." She shrugged and sipped her tea. "You gotta understand," she blurted. Then she stopped. When she continued, her tone was condescending, aloof. "You . . . you must understand. I'm getting an apartment in Manhattan. You have no idea how much I'm growing."

"Go on a diet," he said. Sometimes he didn't know whether she was talking to him or to herself and it bothered him.

"That's why we can only dance together," she said sharply. "Dance but nothing more, nothing personal, no coming on to me."

"Why not?"

"'Cause I don't dig guys like you no more. You're too young; you haven't any class. I'm tired of jerk-off guys who haven't got their shit together."

He almost laughed, but his mouth was full of hamburger. "I got my shit together," he said, storing the meat in his cheek. "It's easy—all you need is a salad bowl and a potato masher."

"Very funny," Stephanie scowled.

"Then why ain't you laughing?"

"Because," she said archly, "I'm one of those people who says 'very funny' instead of laughing."

He washed the second hamburger down with a sip of coffee.

"Hey, you want to know what I do?" he asked seriously.

"It's not necessary."

"I work in a paint store. I got a raise this week."

"Right, you work in a paint store, you probably live with ya . . . your family, you hang out with your buddies and blow it all off Saturday night at 2001."

Tony stared at her, amazed, delighted. "Right!" he said.

"You're a cliché—nowhere, on your way to no place."

"What the hell you got," he demanded, "a stairway to the stars?"

"Maybe. You didn't get any college, did you?"

"No."

"I'm taking a course nights at NYU, two next semester. You ever think about going to college?"

"No," he said angrily.

"Not ever?"

"No! What the fuck you bugging me about it?!"

"Didn't you want to?"

"Fuck off, willya! No! I didn't!"

"Why not?"

"Shit, come off it!" he shouted, glaring at her. "Come off it, would ya!!"

Taken aback by his outburst, Stephanie studied him warily. She sipped her tea quietly while he devoured the last hamburger. He called for the check and walked in front of her to the cashier's counter near the door. Outside, they began walking toward the corner together. Again, they had turned instinctively, without touching or talking. There seemed to be nothing left to say. Finally, Tony broke the silence.

"I want you to know something," he began forcefully. "Something about me and blowing it all off on Saturday night, like you said. There's a high I get that you don't know nothing about . . ."

He was going to tell her how good he was, how great; how he never had to stand in line and chicks got off just wiping his sweat and guys gave him free albums. He was going to impress the hell out of her, but it didn't come out that way. One minute he was saying things just to make points with a snotty stranger, with Stephanie Mangano, and, the next, he was honestly trying to say something—something that he wanted to say almost as much as he wanted her to hear it.

"The high I get at 2001, just dancing, not just being the best . . . I want . . . I wanna get—have—that high someplace else in my life, you know what I mean?"

"Where?"

"I don't know. Somewhere." He couldn't look at her. He shrugged, "I mean it can't last forever. It's a short time thing. You get older. So what does that mean?" he laughed. "Like I ain't never going to feel like that again about anything ever?"

When he did look at her, it was as bad as he'd expected. She looked sad, she looked sorry for him.

"We've got to split here," she said at the corner.

"I'll walk you home."

"No. I'll see you at the studio. I'll dance in the contest with you but nothing personal. Right?" She didn't wait for an answer. She turned the corner and walked away.

He watched her for a little while. He considered the possibility of running after her. Finally, he turned and walked back toward the luncheonette. Half a block down, suddenly, savagely, he kicked out at a wire trash basket. The basket rolled over, spewing garbage into the street. For a minute or so, he stared vacantly at the overturned basket and the scattered trash, then he began to run. He ran home.

Bobby C.'s red Chevy was parked in front of Tony's house. He noticed it as he rounded the corner. The dented front fenders marked it indisputably. He trotted over to the car and peered in. Joey, Double J. and Bobby C. were inside. They looked as though they'd been waiting for him. They looked moody, bored and irritated.

"Where you been?" Joey snapped at him.

"Shove it, Joey," Double J. said, "Hey, Tony, Gus is in the hospital. Some P.R.'s got him."

"Fucking spics!" Joey grumbled.

"Spanish Barons?"

"No. Fucking Barracudas," Double J. said.

"Let's go get them mothers!" Tony opened the front car door and jumped in.

"Hey, nobody's going to be there now," Bobby C. said.

"Check it out," Tony ordered. "Come on. Let's go."

Bobby C. started the car. He didn't seem as enthusiastic as the others—certainly not as hopped up as Joey, who was slamming his fist into his palm while he filled Tony in on what had happened.

"I got to see him in the hospital, you know. Gus, he got a busted rib, busted nose and leg, four teeth knocked out."

"Shit," Tony said. "I seen him a couple hours ago."

"He was carrying home a bag of groceries," Joey continued.

"Yeah, yeah. That's when I seen him!"

"Three of them did a shove number on him and he dropped the fucking groceries . . . spilling all over. All he did, he said, like under his breath, you know, 'spics . . . fuckin' greaseballs'—and they laid into him. Three of them!"

Tony whirled to face Bobby C. "Can't you move

this asshole car? What's the matter with you, man? Drive the fucker, drive!"

"S'matter with me?" Bobby C. rejoindered softly, "Look at you. Why don't you just cool your ass, okay? I'm driving. I'm doing what you fucking told me to."

"Hey, you crazy?" Tony said. "You talkin' to me that way."

Bobby C. lapsed into a brooding silence, which went unnoticed because Joey, Double J. and Tony took up the slack, hyping each other:

"Wreck the greasers!"

"Put it to them!"

"Kick Spic ass, man!"

The volume in the car lowered automatically as the Chevy approached the street on which The Barracudas' club house was located. Bobby C. cruised the block once.

"Go on back, now," Tony ordered. "Once more around only turn your lights off this time."

The Chevy turned into The Barracudas' block again. The club house was a store front. Its window had been painted black and there was a crudely lettered "Members Only" sign taped to the door.

Bobby C. stopped the car a few doors down from the club house and Tony jumped out. Bobby C. had noticed the heavy padlocks on the front door of the club house. Apparently, none of the others had. Double J. and Joey were jiggling around in the back seat, whispering inaudible advice and encouragement to Tony as he crept up to the window of the club house and peered in through a chink in the paint.

"Shit. Nobody there," Tony said, returning to the car.

Bobby C. didn't mention the padlocks. He started the car up and drove off. The others were grim, silent.

"Jesus, you were hot to kick ass," Bobby C. said softly to Tony.

"You guys wait for me, turn me on, now you tell me I got the hots to kick ass!" Tony exploded.

"Hey, listen," Double J. said. "They got thirty, forty members. We jump the place—we get our ears stuffed in our assholes."

"So we keep cruising. We just cruise the place at our pleasure till they got a number we can handle."

"We could just pick off a couple on the street," Bobby C. suggested.

"That's punky," Tony sneered. "P.R. punky."

Bobby C. pulled the Chevy to a stop in front of Tony's house.

"Hey," he called as Tony got out.

Tony walked around to the driver's side. "Yeah?" he said. Bobby C. mumbled something. "What's the matter?" Tony asked.

"I . . . I'm going to, maybe, be getting married," Bobby C. said. It sounded like an apology.

"Fuck that shit, man." Tony said.

"Yeah, can it!" Joey shouted from the back.

"Just thought you guys would want to know is all."

Tony stared curiously at Bobby C. for a second, then he laughed. "Hey listen," he said. "It ever happens, we'll go with you on your honeymoon, okay? Take it easy." He reached through the window and mussed Bobby C.'s hair. "Night." Then he turned quickly and dashed into the house.

Frank Jr. wasn't home, not that night or the next morning when Tony got up. He dressed quickly and ran downstairs. Linda was in the kitchen.

"You seen Frank Jr?" he asked her.

"Mommy says he's staying in your room, ain't he?" she said.

He didn't answer. He heard his father's footsteps overhead, in his room; then his mother's, kind of shuffling around, lost. "See you later, ugly," he said to Linda and left the house.

Lunch time, he went to Shirtown and got the shimmering icy blue shirt. He couldn't stop looking at it. All the way home, that evening, he kept popping the box open, sneaking peeks at it. He ran straight upstairs.

His room was exactly as he'd left it that morning. There was no sign that Frank Jr. had returned.

Disappointed, Tony opened the box and spread the shirt out on the bed. He tried to imagine what Frank would have said about it. Of course, it was kind of slick for a priest, even an ex-priest, but he was sure his brother would have said something nice about it. Jesus, he thought, it felt good just to know there was someone living under your own roof who you could talk to once in a while.

He hung the shirt up in his closet and went downstairs. The family—minus Frank Jr.—was getting ready to eat. Everyone but his grandmother looked tense and gloomy. No one spoke to him when he sat down. He filled his plate with meat loaf and potatoes and reached for the bottle of soda on the table. Linda reached for it at the same time. "Go ahead," he said charitably. She looked at him and burst into tears.

"Hey, what's the matter?" he asked. When Linda didn't answer, he looked around the table at the others.

His mother was staring at him strangely, suspiciously. When she finally spoke, her tone was accusatory. "Tony! What'd you say to Father Frank Jr.?"

"What?" he said, startled.

"What'd you say to him? What'd you do?"

"Yeah," his father said, shaking a fork at him. "What'd you say to your brother?"

"Wait a minute. What are you talking about?"

"I'm talking that you musta said something to him, that's what," Flo said. "You talk to him. He sleeps in your room. Next day he stays out all night and don't come back."

"I didn't say nothing to him," Tony said earnestly.

"A priest staying out all night!" she fumed.

"A priest's a grown up," Tony said. "Anyway, he ain't a priest no more."

"Something you said to him," she accused.

Tony stared at his mother, amazed and furious. "You blaming me 'cause he's not a priest no more."

"You been writing to him?" Frank Sr. demanded.

"Christ, I don't believe this," Tony shouted. "You're trying to hang it on me."

He looked from his mother to his father and back. They almost looked alike. Both of them were hunched over, their faces jutting out at him, pinched tight and angry. But their eyes were sort of unfocused. They were facing him, but not really looking at him. They were asking him questions, but not really hearing him either.

Suddenly, his mother smiled. It was her funny smile, the one she put on for church the same as she'd put on her best kerchief or her expensive fur-collared coat. It was a pious and decorative smile.

"He called though," she said. "He'll be back tonight. Another two days, he'll see he's been wrong . . . a time of trial of the soul. He'll go back to the Church."

"No, he won't! He won't . . . ever!" Tony said, his voice quivering.

"Yes, he will," Flo said calmly, the deluded smile still on her lips. She smiled at each person at the table in turn. She smiled and nodded and, as if she were reciting a litany, she said: "I know he will, I know. I'm so sure. I'm so sure that he will that I ain't told nobody . . . because I know he will. Nobody . . ."

Tony couldn't stand it. She was smiling that crazy faraway smile and not seeing or hearing anything except what she wanted to.

"He won't!" Tony shouted vehemently. "He won't! you ain't got a priest in the family no more. You ain't got no saint, no God no more! No more one saint and some other shit children! No more!"

A stunned silence followed his outburst. Then Flo began to cry, slowly and softly at first, then convulsively in great racking sobs. Tony sagged in his chair. As his anger ebbed, his guilt grew and he could hardly bear to look at his mother. Penitent, helpless, he went to her and touched her shoulder timidly.

"Aw, Ma. Ma, I'm sorry, Ma. Honest . . . I'm sorry."

"Are you, Tony?" Frank Sr. asked sternly, skeptically.

The question stung.

Tony turned to face his father. He saw something he couldn't explain. "What kind of a question . . ." he started to say. He shut up fast.

Frank Sr. looked tough, tough and angry as always, but something else, too. For just a second he had looked . . . what? Sheepish? Sneaky? Scared?! Why had he asked whether Tony was really sorry that he'd made his mother cry? Did Frank Sr. give a damn? He didn't look concerned or caring. What was it that had moved across his angry face like a shadow?

Suddenly Tony began to understand. It came to him like a series of body blows—one, two, three.

One: His father didn't give a shit about his mother's distress. All Frank Sr. cared about was his own endless anger, his infinite misery—and finding a dumping ground for it. Two: What Tony had seen on his father's face was desperation. A furious desperation that the sacred dumping grounds were closing down; that Flo wasn't taking it so good anymore; that Tony was getting high-strung all of a sudden, reacting too quickly and violently. They were forgetting who the boss of the house was. Three: Why had his father asked the pompous question? It was Frank Sr.'s way of dumping what he could while the dumping was good. He had lashed out, as fast and hard as he dared, while Tony's guard was down, while Tony was feeling like a bad son, a bad person. And that was the important part: If Frank could continue to convince him that he was a bad son, Tony would continue to accept the crap—the punishment, accusations, abuse—whatever Frank needed to dump.

Tony turned back to his mother. His hand still rested on her shaking shoulder. He was still trying to apologize, to comfort her. Now he looked at her and tried to remember. Had she ever come to his defense? Had she ever told Frank not to hit, not to yell, not to jump all over her son?

No. Never. Not even the time Frank Sr. had

broken three of his fingers for defending her. Tony's chest felt tight. Even her tears now condemned him, became an offering to his father's wrath. *See how he made me cry, Frank? I proved it for you, he's bad.*

He looked at his father and mother and closed his eyes and he could almost hear them saying: "Our good son has hurt us. Thank God we have a bad one to punish."

He understood it all and he didn't want to. He wanted to forget it.

He breathed deeply. He filled his lungs with air. His chest felt small and cramped. A Face lives by rules, he told himself. Girls you use. Enemies you destroy. Parents you respect. You live by rules, you're safe.

He let the air out and took a new, deeper breath. Parents you respect. His lungs expanded. *Parents you respect.* His chest felt larger. *Parents you respect.* He knew he would forget.

Upstairs he showered and dressed quickly. The shirt was not for tonight but it made him feel good just to see it hanging in his closet. He put the album Paulie had given him on his dresser, then selected four or five others from his collection. When he left the house, he smelled of Brut, his hair was perfect, he had a half dozen dynamite disco albums under his arm, and his head was empty of everything but great expectations.

There was only one problem left to deal with and she was standing in front of Phillips Dance Studios smiling lovingly at him. Tony had forgotten. Annette —eager, glowing, resolved to learn faster and dance better than she ever had in her life—was waiting.

He slowed his pace and gathered his determination. He walked cool and tough and the closer he got, the goddamned brighter she glowed. There was no use telling himself that he was going to do it this way for her sake, straight and fast. He scowled sullenly. It was the only preparation he could think to offer her.

"Look, Annette," he said. "I changed my mind. I got another partner."

Her face collapsed. The smile, the perky tilt of her head, the glow—gone in an instant, replaced by huge, hurt, uncomprehending eyes that misted, brimmed, flooded with tears.

"Look," Tony said quickly. "It's strictly professional. Things like this happen when it's professional."

Annette blinked and the flood-gates opened. Fat tears spilled from her darkly-painted eyes. Mascara and eye liner got caught in the torrent and washed over her cheeks, streaking through the blush-on, leaving her face ashen and wet.

"Jesus Christ!" Tony shouted. "My fucking mother . . . Now you!" He stared at her feeling angrier and more helpless as her sobbing became more violent.

"Why," she gasped hysterically. "Why do you hate me? All I ever did to you is like you!"

Her words startled him. Instinctively, he reached out to calm her, then withdrew his hand, ferociously. Rules, he reminded himself. With a final glance, half-scornful, half-sympathetic, he walked past her into the dance studio.

Pete was at the front desk looking bored.

"Hey, man. Which room you got?" Tony asked.

"Hi, ya. Take number five, it's got a player," Pete said nodding at the records under Tony's arm. "Where's your little friend tonight?"

"What do you mean?" Tony said quickly, defensively.

"That little blonde you was here with Monday. What'd you think I meant?"

"Oh, her. She ain't coming tonight. I got a new partner."

Pete raised his eyebrow quizzically.

"That one I asked you about," Tony explained with reluctance. "You know, that Stephanie one."

Pete's eyebrow stayed up. Something between a leer and a grin crept across his face. "You don't waste time, do you? You making it with her?"

Tony forced himself to return the grin and shrug his shoulders ambiguously. "She's a good dancer," he said. "She here yet?"

"Uh-uh, not yet."

"Okay, well, thanks Pete. I'll wait in the practice room."

"What about the little one with the knockers?" Pete called after him. "I could get off giving her a couple of free lessons."

"Naw, she don't need none," he said. "She's a good dancer, too." He opened the door to the back room.

"Not good enough, though, huh?" Pete yelled. "Not as good as your new friend, the Bay Ridge ball-buster."

Tony walked straight on back to room five. He shuffled through his record albums, chose one, slipped it out of its protective paper sleeve, and studied the sides. Finally, he put the album on the turntable— Side 1 up—and glanced at the door. His face creased with annoyance as he walked across the room and looked out into the empty hallway.

Returning, he switched the record player on. Disco music filled the room. He danced alone for a few seconds then, overcome with anger, crossed the room again to shut the music off.

Stephanie arrived a moment later. She seemed not to know that she was late or that he was steaming about it. What made it worse was that he wasn't sure whether she didn't know or just didn't care.

"Hi," she said coolly.

"You're late."

"Five minutes? That's not late." She hung her coat on a wire hanger behind the door and didn't even look at him. "How long you been here?"

"Six, seven minutes."

"Oh?" she challenged. "Pete said fifteen."

"Fuck him," Tony said. Then, switching the subject, "I brought my own records."

"Great. Let's see." She knelt down and began flipping through the albums. "Super!"

"Super?!" he grumbled and walked past her to the record player. He switched it on again, the same cut he'd been dancing to alone.

She stood up and he turned and all of a sudden they were facing each other and it was time to begin and they couldn't. Each of them looked uncomfortable. Each of them seemed reluctant to surrender the hostility that formed the bedrock of their relationship so far. That sometimes subtle, sometimes crackling, antagonism provided not just a safe distance, but the only common ground they'd established. They had not danced together before. They had never even touched. They had only that comfortable, comforting wariness.

So they stood separately before the mirror, disco music swirling around them, in an otherwise empty room. They faced each other tensely, until they remembered that they wanted something from one another and that, unable to define what it was, they had temporarily settled for a shot at the Sweepstakes together.

Awkwardly, they extended their arms to each other. They touched. Their arms and hands, formal, polite, in dancing position, they began to move to the music. It took only a few bars for their movements and bodies to blend comfortably. They were surprised, pleased, at how well they danced together.

"Wait," Tony said abruptly and stopped. "I want to show you something." He stepped back from her and performed an intricate series of steps. "See. Now here's yours." He demonstrated the woman's moves and then—"I go like this, right,"—his own.

Stephanie watched. Her concentration was total. "That's nice," she said, "that's good."

"Okay, let's try it."

They moved into each other's arms without hesitation and began. It wasn't totally smooth. There were adjustments to make, but after a minor misstep or two, they had incorporated the new steps and were dancing well. Their excitement grew, adding a tension that felt and looked right; a tension that stored and released energy precisely as it was required.

"Yeah, that's good," Stephanie laughed. "You make it up?"

"Yes—no—shit, I saw it on TV, you know."

"Hang on, let me show you one."

She stepped back but before she could begin her demonstration, he shouted, "Wait!" and ran out of the room.

Stephanie waited, hurt and bewildered. She heard his footsteps echo down the corridor, stop, then grow loud again as he returned. The mask of distrust had not quite hardened on her face when he burst back into the room and yanked the record player plug out of the wall socket.

"Grab the albums," he told her. "Come on." He took the record that had been playing and, carrying the phonograph under his arm, hurried out again.

This time she followed him.

He disappeared into a room down the hall. When she caught up, she discovered a practice studio at least twice the size of the one they had been using. Mirrors on two walls made it appear almost as large as a small ballroom. Tony, with lightning speed, had finished setting up the record player. He threw the switch and stood up as music filled the awesome space. The small speakers crackled. He adjusted the volume until the sound was right and the speakers free of static. Then he turned to her, smiling.

"Now," he said.

She moved into his arms and they began to dance.

"Wait." She interrupted to show him her step.

"Oh, yeah," he said warmly. "Let's do it."

There was no faltering this time. They knew each other's bodies and anticipated each other's movements with stunning accuracy. They drifted from her step back to the series he had taught her. They became innovative together. The excitement of the dance, of performance and creativity, was suddenly inseparable from their delight with one another.

They worked at it. They played at it. They traded routines. They were wet with perspiration and oblivious of the time when Pete rapped at the door.

"Very nice," he said with genuine enthusiasm. "I hate to bust it up, honest, but I got a class in this room 'bout five minutes." He crossed to the record player and switched it off. "Anyways, you don't want to run it into the ground, do you? Two and a half hours . . . I ain't going to be able to spare that every night."

Stephanie and Tony looked at each other, surprised that so much time had passed. Then, suddenly, Pete's intrusion and the absence of the music overwhelmed them. They dropped hands and turned away from one another.

"I better go get my coat," Stephanie said. She tossed her head back energetically and rubbed her neck. When she noticed that Tony and Pete were staring at her, she straightened abruptly, assumed her cool and dignified posture, and left the room.

"Wow, Pete . . . two and a half hours," Tony said, gathering the albums together. "Didn't seem that long. Sorry about the room."

"No problem, kid," Pete waved the apology away magnanimously. "You two looked dynamite."

Tony slipped the last record they'd used back into its cover.

"You going to take the player back to room five, right?"

"Sure," Tony agreed. He wrapped the cord around the phonograph and hoisted the box up under his arm. "Okay, well, see you," he said. Then he just stood there. He wasn't quite ready to go back to the little practice room. Stephanie would be there—that other Stephanie, the one he had never danced with. That's how she'd looked when she left to get her coat, as if they'd never touched one another. He felt tired, slowed down, which was strange because dancing usually gave him energy, an extra charge, a high.

He walked to the door feeling strangely somber. Something had happened between them. Goddamn it, he thought, he *knew,* something really nice had gone down. When they were dancing, she was all loose and easy and laughing. She responded to every move he made. She followed him.

He heard her coming down the corridor.

"I'm going to unload this," he told her about the

record player, "then I'll meet you downstairs, okay?"

"It's okay, you don't have to," she said.

"I want to. Would you just wait a minute? I mean, just let me unload this. Just take a second."

He took the record player back to the little practice room, pulled his leather jacket off the hook where he'd hung it and went back out into the corridor. Stephanie was standing at the door to the large studio, right where he'd left her. She began to walk as he headed toward her. He slipped into his jacket and caught up to her.

In the street, they walked together slowly, quietly, keeping a discreet distance between them. He felt his energy returning. It came in waves every time he remembered what dancing with her had been like. She wasn't loose and easy now, but she wasn't as self-consciously aloof as she'd been the other evening either.

They reached the corner and stopped automatically.

"Coffee?"

After some hesitation, Stephanie shrugged. "I don't know," she said softly.

"A drink?"

"Okay. No, no. I . . . I think I'll just go home."

Neither of them moved or spoke for a moment. Finally, Tony said, "You know, I like you better this way—when you're all quiet, when you don't lay all that shit on me." He started walking again, slowly. Stephanie kept pace beside him.

"As a matter of fact," she said, "guess who I had lunch with today? Paul Anka!"

Well, at least he knew who Paul Anka was. "Oh yeah?" he said, "Is he having your baby?"

She didn't even smile. "He was very, very, really interesting," she said. "Interesting. Really intelligent and very interesting."

"Interesting . . . interesting, you really cream over that word," Tony muttered. "Interesting!" He pronounced it with distaste. "You know what I've

been thinking," he said after a pause. "I've been thinking . . . I've been thinking, maybe, you're full of shit's
what I've been thinking. Interesting, ain't it?"

Stephanie smiled with elaborate coolness. "Is that
so?"

"Only I'm not sure," Tony continued. "I'm not so
sure how much of it's shit and how much of it's bullshit. Probably most."

"You hope."

"Hey, we haven't talked about the dancing," he
said abruptly. "You know, like how it felt."

She didn't say anything and they walked along
in silence for awhile.

"We're going to have to keep practicing, of course
he ventured. "Practice a couple more times, and we
ought to try dancing some at 2001 with a crowd . . .
like this Saturday."

"Maybe," she said, "I don't know."

"Hey, listen," he began. Then he laughed. "Hey,
you think I'm either . . . either interesting or intelligent?"

Stephanie looked at him, first to determine whether he was serious or not, then to display a weighty
consideration of the matter. Finally, she said, "Interesting? Yes. Intelligent? Maybe. I'd have to know
you better. You've got a way of seeing things, of putting things together. Yeah . . . maybe interesting and,
yeah, maybe . . . intelligent."

Tony was astonished. And speechless. They
walked another half block in silence. At the corner,
Stephanie stopped. "Goodnight," she said, "thanks."

"I can walk you the rest of the way," he offered.
"You want me to?"

She said no gently, and walked away.

Some distance from him, she turned. He was still
there, watching her. "You shouldn't have asked," she
shouted to him. "You should have just done it!"

He took one step toward her, but she turned
and ran so he stopped and just watched until she was
out of sight.

Saturday night promised to be one of the best. 2001 Odyssey was filled, frenzied and in full tilt, echoing Tony's excitement and expectations. Frank Jr. was with him, and wearing civies, too. The new clothes Frank had bought were conservative and loose-fitting and he hadn't traded in his seminary shoes yet. But, as he'd reminded Tony, it was his first civilian outfit in years and, if the shirt was a quiet cotton, at least the collar buttoned down, not up.

Frank Jr. had admired Tony's new shirt, as had Double J. and Joey and Bobby C., who had spent most of the ride excusing themselves and elbowing each other and, in general, acting like born losers in the Choirboy of the Year competition. Not even their antic behavior, however, could limit Tony's enthusiasm for the evening, so pleased was he that Frank had wanted to come along.

They were in the red-on-red entryway now. As they passed through the crowd at the ticket seller's table Frank Jr. said, "You guys sure have a Moses effect. You arrive—and the crowd parts like the Red Sea."

"Yeah, they know us here." Tony said modestly, but his grin made it obvious that he was pleased Frank had noticed and was impressed.

He led the way to the reserved table, acknowledging greetings en route, nodding his head just a little less curtly than usual, smiling just a little more. As he walked through the busy table area, he scanned the room for Stephanie. He didn't see her, but the place was amazingly jammed and the lights, for this number, were shooting around too rapidly to pick a face out of the crowd.

They sat down and beckoned the waitress. There was a vague uneasiness at the table, a shifting of eyes and bodies, as they waited for Frank Jr. to order. When he decided on scotch, the Faces relaxed a bit. Bobby C. pulled out his sketch pad and began to draw. Double J. leaned back casually and scanned the upper tiers, winking graciously at a table of girls who had begun to fidget and whisper when the Faces walked in.

Frank Jr. had a faint smile on his lips as he scrutinized the place. The lights and music were astounding. He peered through the rainbow haze at the dancers. Their vitality amused and pleased him. He enjoyed the inexhaustible energy and excitement.

The Faces were still subdued. They were unusually quiet and self-conscious tonight. They began and ended sentences abruptly, arbitrarily, so that either no one at the table was speaking or two people would speak rapidly together and each fade out before a single thought developed. There were only a series of awkward sounds, beginnings and endings, but no one actually said anything.

Tony studied his brother's face anxiously, trying to interpret the meaning of his smile. But it was Joey who finally turned to Frank Jr. and said, cautiously, "Well, what do you think, Father? How do you like it?"

Tony glanced sharply at Joey. He was annoyed that Joey had dared, that Joey had asked the question that should have been his. He was relieved, too. The fact was, he'd been reluctant to ask outright; as fearful of a piously bland reaction as he was of outright disapproval.

Frank Jr. smiled indulgently. "Look, I asked you guys before—please don't call me Father. I never could stand that."

Joey dipped his head apologetically and settled into a gloomy silence.

"But, yeah," Frank Jr. continued, "I think it's . . . I think the place is terrific."

Tony straightened up. He nodded to each of the Faces in turn, an unabashed I-told-you-so grin lighting his face.

"Hey, really, that's great!" Joey shouted, released from his self-imposed penance.

"Yeah, yeah!" Double J. agreed. "It really is. Big, you know. Easy to dig."

"Something else, ain't it. It moves. It really moves!"

Then, just as suddenly as their exuberance exploded, it ended. There was silence at the table again. For a moment, the Faces were confused and disappointed by the setback. Then, studying one another and reassuring themselves that Frank Jr. did actually like the place and was still looking around and enjoying himself, they accepted the silence as merely circumstantial; a coincidence and not a soundless indictment. They began, slowly, to loosen up and even to make small talk.

Joey was looking at one of Bobby C.'s drawings, trying to guess which dancer it was supposed to be. "That's the one, over there alone? Looks like her except for the skirt. She's got pants on, man. You just invent that skirt?"

"Ain't her," Bobby C. said. He flipped a page of his pad back and showed it to Joey. "It's the one dancing with him."

"Shit, that's good," Joey said sincerely. "Where'd you learn to draw spades like that? Now I see her. Sure, she's wearing a skirt . . . the one that's dancing with the black dude."

"Where?" Double J. demanded. Then he tapped Tony's arm. "Hey, check it out," he whispered. He tilted his glass toward the dance floor, toward the black and white couple they had seen the week before.

"Cool it," Tony cautioned. His eyes darted to Frank Jr. to see if his brother had heard or reacted to the exchange.

Frank was looking at Bobby C.'s sketch pad. "You've got talent," he said enthusiastically. "What do you do?"

"I fix things—you know, stereos, radios, TV once in awhile."

Frank Jr. shook his head. "You've got real talent. You ought to do something with it. Didn't you ever think about studying art seriously?"

"Aw, one fu . . . one teacher I had, I showed him some stuff, a couple drawings. He said, sure. He didn't even believe I did them. Then he said they was probably all I could do. Once I asked my old man to pay for lessons, you know, art school—one year, one fu . . . one term even. He said I was off my nut."

Frank shook his head. "Amazing," he mumbled. He lifted his glass and downed the scotch almost angrily then he stared off at the dance floor.

Tony was puzzled. Then suddenly, he thought he knew why his brother had become sad and silent. Even he could connect up what had happened to Frank Jr. with what had happened to Bobby C.'s teachers and parents. Frank had said it the other night —*they turn you into what they want at a time when you can't defend yourself against their fantasies. . . .*

Tony felt like shit. He'd known Bobby C. forever, seen him doodling and drawing forever, and he'd never really commented or complimented him on his talent. Even the word had come from his brother: talent! How weird, the two of them sitting now, almost side by side: Frank Jr. and Bobby C. One on his way into the trap. The other escaping. God help him, he was so proud of his brother. God help Bobby C.

"You as good in bed as you are on the dance floor?"

Stunned, Tony spun toward the emphatically feminine, low-pitched voice. It emanated from a lazy-eyed girl who was staring down at him over a pair of impressive breasts cantilevered in red satin. He was too embarrassed, for Frank's sake, to say a word.

"Well, are you?" the girl persisted. "You as good in bed as you are on the dance floor?"

"He never made it in a bed!" Joey cracked. Then he glanced uneasily at Frank Jr. who, it turned out, had heard the entire exchange and was working at keeping a growing grin in check.

Tony stood up abruptly and grabbed the girl's waist. "Uh, this ain't my real partner," he said to Frank

Jr. "She's coming later . . . but watch, okay." He led the girl to the dance floor as fast as her alarmingly high heels permitted.

She was a disappointing dancer, sloppy, knowing the steps but executing them without passion or finesse.

"When do I get my answer?" she teased.

"If you're as good in bed as you are on the dance floor, you're one lousy fuck."

She laughed aloud in that foggy, confident voice. "So how come I get the flowers the next day?"

"Some guys don't recognize a lousy fuck when they get one," he suggested. "Or maybe they just thought you were dead."

In spite of the girl's lackluster performance, Tony managed to manipulate her firmly enough to keep her from faltering seriously. He used her as a prop, working around, rather than with, her. He used her as a foil to his own dazzling spins and steps. He hoped Stephanie Mangano would show up soon.

"He's a good dancer," Frank Jr. said enthusiastically.

"He's the king, Father!" Joey decreed, "Uh . . . man," he corrected himself quickly. "He's the king around here, man. You see him out there? The king."

One of the fidgety girls from the table on the upper tier came down the steps and over to Double J. Without a word and not much more than a glance at her, he got up and walked to the dance floor. The girl smiled and followed gratefully.

Bobby C. slid over into Double J.'s vacated chair. "Uh, Father . . ." he said, drawing water circles on the table with his finger, "I mean, you know, Frank. Something I gotta ask you. Pauline, this girl, I think maybe I knocked her up."

Frank Jr. turned to look at him but Bobby C.'s concentration on the circles was total.

"Pauline, she's a good Catholic," he continued. "She loves the taste of Communion wafers. She says, you know, like the Pope gives special dispensations for divorce for some people. Well, maybe, you know, the Pope would give a dispensation for an abortion."

"I don't think so, Bobby," Frank Jr. said.

"Yeah, well . . . like thanks." He slid back to his own seat and resumed sketching.

Tony and the red-breasted girl were still dancing. He'd shove her forward for a spin and turn his head away from her to peer over his own shoulder at the crowd. The floor was packed, but room always opened around him. He could see girls looking at him behind their partner's backs or sometimes, two girls working out a number together would turn their heads simultaneously, as if staring at him was part of their routine. Sometimes he'd catch a guy watching his moves and, a minute later, trying them out. He saw everything over his shoulder but Stephanie.

The dancers stepped and counted and spun. She was not among them. The music was loud and heavy on the bass beat. Every once in a while, a whiff—like stale socks—floated by on someone who'd just done a popper. The unmistakable stench of amyl nitrate mingled with sweat and Brut and Love—the cologne, not the emotion.

"Hello again, this is beautiful Bernie, your delirious DJ!" The voice crackled over the music. "Reminding you that the All-Brooklyn Universal Disco Sweepstakes is only a week away. And also to remind you that anything you feel out there—ecstacy, rapture, euphoria, high, spacy, freaky—is 'cause of the way I flip the discs, needle the grooves, hit the bands, phase in, phase out, from which to what and where to there. Taking you where you want to be but can't get by yourself. For I am wizard and magician, Merlin and Svengali . . . and you, you are my gnomes!"

A theatrical cackle concluded the disc jockey's power trip. It was followed by a scattered but emphatic chorus of "fuck you's" from the dance floor which inspired one last sinister laugh from the disc jockey. He then unleashed a thunderously loud finale of the music that had backed his spiel.

Tony left the dance floor. The DJ's reminder that the Sweepstakes was only a week away had soured him. He used the subsequent rowdiness, the hoots and catcalls of the crowd and Bernie's fiddling with the volume, as an excuse—an affront to his dignity as a serious dancer. He left the girl and he left the ballroom and, without knowing why, he walked past the bar to the entranceway.

There were still people waiting to get in. Tony scanned the line accepting some greetings with a minimal smile, nodding to those he considered worthier. Most of the faces were familiar. None were exciting.

A guy in a shiny blue suit was helping the ticket seller check customers in. He was the bouncer, and big. He stood beside the admissions table with his hands behind his back just nodding his consent when someone who'd gone out for awhile returned. Tony had seen those hands. They were probably behind the guy's back because they wouldn't fit into his pockets and he probably needed a license to carry them anyway. He almost always wore the same suit—dark blue flashing to purple depending on the light, a little too tight across the chest but always immaculate. Tony had seen him handle two speed-freaky punks one night without wrinkling the suit. That was the night he'd first noticed the big guy's hands.

"Hi ya, Tony," the girl at the table said. "You going out for awhile?"

"Maybe. Hey, you know Stephanie Mangano?" he said with studied cool.

"No."

"I do," the guy with the hands said.

"You see her tonight? She come in?"

"No."

"Yeah, well, okay then. Thanks." He nodded to the ticket seller and the bouncer and walked back toward the ballroom. He was halfway to the table, when he saw his brother coming toward him.

"Hey, Tony."

"Hi, ya. Were you looking for me?"

"Yes," Frank Jr. said. "I'm going home."

"Oh wow, what for?" Tony felt his heart sink. "Why don't you stay a little longer?"

"It's not my scene, you know. You didn't expect me to stay the whole night, did you?"

Tony looked down and shook his head. "No . . . yes . . . I, uh. No, no, I guess not. Of course this isn't your kind of scene."

"You're a marvelous dancer," Frank Jr. said. "It's exciting to watch you."

"Yeah, well, thanks."

They walked toward the door straining at the silence that had fallen between them.

"I'm glad you asked me to come," Frank said.

"Just as well you're going. . . ." Tony spoke at the same time, then he and Frank smiled at the coincidence.

"If you stayed, they'd probably blame me," Tony continued, "You know, Ma and Pa, they'd figure I was leading you to a life of sin." It was supposed to be a joke, but he hadn't the heart for it.

"That the way it was last time?" Frank Jr. asked.

"What do you mean?"

"The other night when I didn't come home. Did they blame you?"

"No. They acted like I was supposed to know. Like I hid you away or something."

"When I called Ma, I told her. I looked up a friend from the seminary. This guy Tommy Noonan. I ever mention him to you? Well, he got me in touch with this group, a group of ex-priests. You believe that?" Frank laughed. "They got a group, a national organization, full of dropouts just like me. Over in Manhattan. They've got active priests, too, working along with them. Anyway, it seems that everyone goes through the same thing, same problems—dealing with parents, family, old friends, facing the Church again, facing yourself. I stayed over there and then I went to see this job counselor. He works with them, too."

"You gonna get a regular job?"

"You didn't know? How come they didn't tell you—Ma, Pa? How come you didn't ask me?"

Tony shrugged.

"Listen, Tony, we've got a lot to catch up on and practically no time. I'm sorry, honest, I am. But I . . . not here, I can't talk now, here. When you get home tonight. Or else, first thing in the morning. Okay?"

Frank Jr. put his hand on Tony's shoulder as they continued toward the door.

"You know what? You're about to lose your title, champ," he said jokingly. But there was an undercurrent of seriousness, melancholy, in his tone. "I hate to do it to you, kid, but I'm taking over as The Shame of the Manero's and, God help you, they'll probably start depending on you to make them proud."

"Hey, come on. What are you talking about?"

"Tomorrow," Frank Jr. said very softly. They'd reached the entrance. Beyond the waiting crowd, they embraced.

"I'm glad I got a chance to see you dance. See you later, okay?"

"Yeah, sure." *If Stephanie'd been here,* he thought *you'd have stayed longer and you'd have really seen me dance.* "See you," he said and walked back inside.

He paused at the admissions table. "She come in yet?"

The bouncer blinked at him. "You were just here."

"Right, right," Tony said angrily; then he smiled a big, friendly grin that was supposed to mean, "no hard feelings, huh?" and, retrieving his composure, strolled into the ballroom.

The anger stayed with him, though.

He explained Frank's disappearance to the Faces at the table. "He didn't feel too good, got sick or something."

"Too bad," Joey said—but he seemed relieved, relaxed finally.

"You want to get that black fuck out of here now?" Double J. said. They were all relieved and glad to be getting down to business as usual.

"You kidding," Tony was grateful for the chance to work off his anger. "Yeah!"

Double J. moved out into the aisle. The others stood, too. But as they started toward the dance floor, Tony, in the lead, stopped them abruptly.

"Jesus fuckin' Christ!" he moaned.

Two burly locals had just closed in on the black guy. They pinned him between them and jabbing and shoving, they worked him toward the door.

"Shit," Joey said. "They stole our fucking act."

Double J. shot him a suspicious glance. "You really sorry, right? Now Bobby C. can't impress you with his fuckin' African artwork no more."

Bobby C. blinked. "What'd I do, man?"

"He draws good. What the fuck's with you?" Joey demanded.

Double J.'s fist were pumping impotently. For a minute it looked like he might hang Joey off the end of one of them. Tony grabbed Double J.'s arm and punched it, harder than the playful tap it appeared. "You want to be cool out there," he told him. "You want to move back to the table with respect."

Double J. ripped his arm away from Tony. "Sure," he said, working on a grin. "Sure. What are we standing here decorating the stairs for anyway? The fucker's gone."

Frustrated and sullen, they returned to their table.

Tony was staring out at the dance floor—past the floor, really, toward the entrance—when Annette appeared. He didn't see her, just felt her plump perfumed presence beside him; and he didn't look up when she spoke.

"Tony? I got to speak to you." She sounded nervous. No petulance, no demands in her voice, only an imploring quaver.

"Yeah?" he stared straight ahead.

"We could make it now."

"What?" he said, and spun to face her.

"Uh, we ain't practicing, seeing each other like you said . . . so we could make it."

She kneeled toward him slightly. Her hands rested on her knees for balance. Her breasts, pressed between her bare arms, were almost totally exposed as if she had deliberately struck the pose to accentuate her words. But the shakiness in her voice was just plain scared.

"I told you . . ." he began irritably. "Hey, fix up your blouse. What's the matter with you, the way you're hanging out, there . . . I told you when we make it, it's because I decide."

She stood up and straightened the neckline of her dress, then squinted at him shyly. "Okay," she said, her tone reedy but braver, "then, I'll just make it with somebody else."

He laughed at her. "Yeah, who?"

"Anybody. Somebody here. I . . . I don't care!"

"Somebody here!" he said angrily.

"Sure," she said, picking up momentum, strength, from his incredulous look. "Sure. Double J., Joey . . ."

The evening's disappointments, frustrations, welled up in him once more. Frank Jr. had left too early. Stephanie had not shown up at all. His black prey had been ripped off. And now, Annette was threatening him. She was threatening him! He could feel his cool slipping. His fury breaking through.

"The fuck you will!" he hissed at her. He grabbed her arm, pinching it tightly. He pulled himself to his feet using her arm as a lever. "The fuck you going to screw around with my head! Let's go!" He dragged her a few paces then turned. "Hey, you creeps," he called out to the Faces, "We're going to the car. This ain't going to take no time. We'll go up on the bridge soon as I'm done."

He dragged her to the door of the discotheque. She was whimpering a little, but he held her and she ran awkwardly on her toes to keep up the pace he set. Outside, he let go of her and walked ahead to the car. She followed, hobbling, running, rubbing her bruised arm. He left the rear door open for her. When she climbed in, he was leaning up against the far corner of the back seat waiting.

She closed the door and wriggled across the seat to him. He stared over her head at the window.

"Oh, Tony," she sighed romantically. She put her arms around his neck and kissed him and, at the touch of his hand on the small of her back, she thrust herself forward.

He couldn't find her dress zipper, so he moved his hands to her thighs and pushed her dress up while she kept kissing and pressing him up against the armrest. He tugged at her panties. She sucked at his neck.

"Cut that out, you crazy?" he said, pulling away.

"M'sorry," she whispered and stopped sucking at his neck. Her lips moved up, her hands moved down. She fondled him. He fingered her.

"Oh please, now," she begged him.

"You done this before?" he said suspiciously.

"Never, Tony. Honest, I swear."

He kissed her and pulled her panties off.

She was struggling to unfasten his belt. He pushed her hand away and opened it himself and unzipped his fly while she kissed his ear and jaw and lips and fastened like a homing leech onto his neck again.

"You fixed?" he asked.

"What do you mean?" she whispered.

"You know, birth control."

"No," she mumbled into his neck.

He pulled her away from him and held her by the shoulders, staring at her in astonishment. "No pill?"

She shook her head miserably, "No."

"Nothing inside . . . like, you know, those fuckin IOU's or whatever?"

"No, no, no."

He sat up abruptly.

"Tony, Tony, I love you," she pleaded.

"Shit," he said, zipping up his fly. "You ought to meet Bobby C.'s girlfriend, Pauline."

He turned away from her and looked out the window. The Faces were heading toward the car. "Oh Shit!" he said. "Okay, okay, on the road!" he called to them. And to Annette, who was huddled in the far corner, he said softly, "Like everything's cool. That's how you act, okay!"

The Faces tumbled into the car. They were loud and laughing and working hard at building the rhythm they'd need to sustain them at the bridge. Bobby C. started the car and pulled away from the curb with unusual recklessness.

Tony glanced at Annette. She was combing her hair. Her head was down so he couldn't see her face but, then, neither could Double J., who'd joined them in the back seat, or the others in the car.

"You ready to get it on?" Joey called to Tony.

"Give the guy a break," Double J. urged. "He fuckin' just got it off!"

"Turn on the radio, would ya?" Annette said.

Bobby C. switched it on. A newscast was in progress. Joey reached forward to change the station even before Tony hollered, "Aw shove it. Find some music."

"There was a flood in Bay Ridge, Brooklyn today . . ." Joey mimicked the voice of the bored newscaster as he turned the dial.

"Yeah, in the back seat of Bobby C.'s Chevy," Double J. hooted.

"Twenty-seven persons were killed . . ." Bobby C. intoned gravely.

Double J. winked at Tony. "Yeah. All of them, unborn!"

"Oh fucking mother of Christ, what am I going to do?!" Bobby C. wailed.

"You're going to watch where the hell you're driving, asshole! Slow down, man. You almost missed the turnoff."

"You going up on the Verrazano?" Annette asked.

"You know a better place?" Tony said.

"For what?"

"For fly . . .ying!" Joey sang out.

"Or swimming," Double J. added sinisterly. You want to go for a swim? Take a look. It's the high dive, man. You want to try it?"

"She don't try nothing," Tony warned. "She can sit in the car. This ain't for chicks."

They were on the approach ramp to the upper roadway of the Verrazano Narrows Bridge. It loomed before them, shimmering silver, arching breathtakingly two hundred feet above the black water. On the other side, the shoreline of Staten Island was articulated by thousands of tiny dots—pinpoints of light. Viewed in the distance from the height of the bridge, cars cruising the bank looked like battery-run toys; their white headlights and red taillights like twin streaks in the darkness.

Midway across the bridge, Bobby C. slowed the car and pulled over to the side. Before he snapped the motor off, Joey, Double J. and Tony leaped out onto the upper roadway. Joey got to the railing first. He climbed up on it, grabbed a cable, and swung out into space. For a moment, he hung suspended, the full weight of his body sustained by the thick metal cable. He howled at the top of his lungs. The sound echoed insanely in the night. Then the cable snapped back and returned him to the railing and he jumped onto the bridge with his arms outstretched and his mouth still open.

Annette, horrified, stared out the window as Tony took Joey's place on the railing. She clutched the little golden cross at her neck and pressed her fists against her throat, as if to suppress a scream. As Tony leaped from the railing, she tightened her grasp on the cross and its points cut into her palms. She closed her eyes and prayed fervently. When she opened them again, Tony was sailing back toward the bridge, sailing two hundred feet above the world at a spectacular speed, back to safety.

Double J. was perched on the railing, ready, waiting. Bobby C. stood in the shadow of one of the girders, watching silently. Joey stood a few feet back from the edge, catching his breath, laughing, welcoming Tony back to earth.

Annette clutched the little cross and watched Double J. swing out on the cable. As the others had, he grasped the cable with his whole body; hands, arms, thighs, chest, calves. He soared Tarzan-like through the void. Then, at the apex of the cable's arch, he released his body grasp and held on only with his hands.

On the bridge, Tony and Joey cheered and stomped. "Come on, motherfucker. Bring it home!" "I'm next, you crazy son-of-a-bitch! Watch this one!"

Suddenly Annette ran hysterically from the car. "Stop it! Stop it! I can't watch anymore!"

She ran to the railing and looked down. Impulsively Tony grabbed her arm. "Oh my God," she gasped as she calculated the drop and the suicidal chances they had taken. "Oh Jesus Christ, no! Stop it! Stop it!" she begged.

Tony, Double J. and Joey laughed. They were elated. They were giddy with power and pride at the recklessness of their performance. Annette's hysteria was a heady tribute. Tony released her arm and she backed away from them, sobbing. Still excited and laughing, they followed her to the car.

When they were all back inside, Joey turned suddenly to Bobby C.

"Now, what about you?"

Bobby C. turned the motor on. "I'm driving," he said softly.

In the back seat, Double J. and Tony hadn't heard the exchange. They were congratulating themselves and each other and taunting Annette by describing how close they had come to the ultimate rush—letting go.

She was still pale and shaky when Bobby C. stopped the car in front of her house. She stared at them, examining each of their faces through dazed, wondering eyes. She seemed not to recognize them, not even Tony. Then she got out of the car and walked away without saying a word, without turning to look at them again.

"Want to cruise The Barracudas club house?" Double J. asked as they drove off.

"I'm tired," Bobby C. said. "Anyways, it's late. Ain't any of them going to be there anyway."

"You tired?" Double J. snapped. "How you think Gus's feeling tonight?"

"Poor bastard," Joey said.

"Yeah. And he could have run, you know. He could have, but he didn't. He hung tight."

"Bobby C.'s right," Tony said. "It's too late tonight. We'll tear the spicdicks up, Double J. We ain't forgetting Gus. But I gotta get home now. Something important I've got to talk to my brother about."

But it was too late for that, too.

Frank Jr. was sound asleep. Tony undressed quickly and quietly, put out the light Frank had left on for him, and lay down on the mattress beside the bed. He lay awake in the dark for awhile. Something about the room wasn't quite right, but he didn't want to get up or put the light on again.

He couldn't figure it out. Then, suddenly, he was too tired. It was something important, he knew, but he was just too tired to figure it out.

When he woke, the room was flooded with daylight and Frank Jr. was up, dressed, and leaning over him.

"I was just going to wake you. I wanted to before, but you were really out. I shook you a couple of times, then I figured you needed the rest."

Tony sat up. He knew what was wrong. He knew what hadn't been right about the room last night. He felt sick, breathless.

Just behind Frank Jr., next to the door, there

were two suitcases. They were standing upright. They were black. They were Frank's. Tony couldn't be certain whether he'd noticed them there last night, or only that they were not in the bottom of the closet when he'd hung up his clothes. But that was what had bothered him—that the closet hadn't seemed full enough, or the dresser as cluttered as it should have been. The room had felt strange and empty last night and now he knew why.

"You're leaving," he said.

"Yes."

"You should have woke me. When you going?"

"Soon as you get dressed and walk me down to the car." Frank Jr. said apologetically.

"You should have woke me," Tony repeated helplessly.

"I tried. Come on, Tony. I want you to walk out with me. You know Tommy Noonan I told you about? He's here. He's waiting outside for me. I want you to meet him. I've told him about you."

"Where you going?"

"I got a job in a settlement house. Starts tomorrow. Tommy's giving me a lift over."

"Gee, that's great," Tony said.

"You going to get dressed or you going to meet Noonan in your shorts?"

"One minute." He got up quickly and dressed. Frank sat on the bed.

"Where's Ma?" Tony asked, zipping up his trousers hurriedly.

"They're in church. All of them."

"They know?"

Frank Jr. nodded, yes. "Ma wanted to stay home. I asked Pa not to let her. They all know. They think Grandma doesn't, but she does. She kissed me as they were leaving and she whispered, '*Buone fortuna . . . Fata di forata.*'—luck and courage! And they're afraid to tell her."

Tony smiled. "Okay, I'm ready."

Outside, a car was waiting at the curb. There

was a man about Frank Jr.'s age behind the wheel. When he saw them coming, he got out of the car and walked around to the trunk.

"Tommy," Frank Jr. said, "this is my kid brother, the dancer. Tony, meet Tommy Noonan, friend to the fallen."

"Hi, ya." Noonan said and took the suitcases from Frank and put them in the trunk.

"Why don't you stay longer?" Tony said. He couldn't look right at Frank and he couldn't not say it either.

"Ex-priests don't stay back at home. Everyone's too shocked, disgraced. Tell him, Tommy," Frank Jr. urged.

"A family raises a priest, they think they've scored points in heaven. Your folks, now they think they're going to lose their points . . ." Noonan smiled and climbed back into the car.

"Hey, we'll keep in touch," Frank said with sudden enthusiasm.

"Yeah, that'll be great. You going to like this settlement house stuff?" Tony asked.

"It'll do until I've figured out my next move. How about you? You know, you were so good last night. You really should do something with your dancing."

"I don't know. Once I thought like opening a dance studio—people ask me—but shit. . . ." He looked away. "All my life I've been hearing I'm no good in the family, no good, no smarts in school . . . nothing like you. Not good, not smart, not a jock, nothing. Fucking nothing! How do you find out you can do anything when all you've heard was that? Nothing. It's hard to try anything new, you know, like opening up a dance studio."

Frank Jr. took his arm. "Hey, look at me, would you? Listen to me." Tony couldn't face him. "Tony, you know the only way you're going to survive is to do what you think you want to do, not what everybody keeps trying to jam you into. Let them do that, you're going to be nothing but miserable."

"Like you, right?"

"Yeah," Frank Jr. said slowly, "like me."

Finally Tony looked at him again. "You, Frank —you're going to end up something else. Why can't I?"

"Who says you can't?"

Tony shrugged.

"Hey," Frank Jr. embraced him, hugged him once, then held him back for a last good look. "I left you something. In your room—a souvenir." Then he turned quickly and got into the car.

Tony watched them drive off. He stood at the curb and watched until, two blocks away, the car turned left and drove out of sight. Then he walked slowly back to the house.

It was unusually quiet, even for a normal Sunday. He looked into the living room, considered checking the coffee situation in the kitchen—sometimes his mother left a pot on the stove for him— decided against it and headed upstairs, instead. He was halfway up when something he had seen peripherally, noticed but not taken note of, piqued his curiosity and he went back down. From the foyer, he peered into the living room again. He looked at the top of the TV console. Frank Jr.'s ordination photograph was gone. The portrait of Frank Jr. in his priest's vestments, as Father Frank Jr., was gone.

The photograph's departure seemed somehow more significant than the man's. It gave Tony a funny feeling. He wanted to roar something, and he wasn't sure whether it would sound like laughter or anguish but he was certain that Frank Jr. would have understood.

He ran up the stairs to his room. The mattress was on the floor and there was no longer any reason for it to be so he began to strip the linens off it. He folded the extra blanket and was about to put it back up on the shelf of his closet when he saw the souvenir.

His brother's clerical collar was lying on the dresser.

Tony walked over and picked up the collar. With a gentle smile, he held the collar up, then wrapped it around his neck and studied himself in the mirror. Then, suddenly, his smile faded. He began to pull the collar tighter and tighter around his neck and tighter still, until it choked him. The priest's collar, the pious symbol, the last vestige of his brother's purity and superiority, choked him—as it never, ever could again.

Finally, he released the collar and took a long, deep breath. For several seconds he stood breathing deeply and staring at the collar. Then he picked it up with great gentleness and tucked it away in the bottom drawer of the dresser.

Dinner was early as usual on Sunday. The silence at the table was formidable but not as oppressive as some of the agitated silences that had existed during the days following Frank Jr.'s return. There was an air of resignation; temporary, perhaps, but certainly a time out for healing seemed to have been called.

At one point, his mother snuffled loudly and pulled a balled-up tissue from the pocket of her house dress. His father shot her a fierce warning look and she responded with quick irritation: "I got a cold. Okay with you I blow my nose?!"

His father, eyes narrowed, face flushed with anger, let it go.

Frank Jr.'s name was not mentioned but, when his mother left the table to carry some dishes to the kitchen, his father turned to him and said sharply: "You here when he took off?"

Tony nodded.

"Okay, then," his father said, as if the answer satisfied him.

Later, upstairs, he ran into Linda in the hallway.

"I wish he could have stayed," she said. It sounded more romantic than sincere. It also made Tony realize that, somehow, he'd become the one person in the house with whom the topic of Frank Jr. could be acceptably broached.

"He leave you anything, in your room, like?" Linda asked.

Tony blanched. The possibility that Frank had mentioned the souvenir to their kid sister, broken some sacred bond between them, hurt bitterly. Maybe, she had seen the collar on the dresser before he woke, before church. Maybe Frank Jr. had left Linda a souvenir, too.

"Why?" he asked.

"I don't know," she responded. "Just 'cause he stayed in your room, you know. I thought if maybe he left something, like a medal or a crucifix or rosary or something and you didn't want it, I thought maybe I could have it. He's my brother, too, you know."

"No," Tony said, relieved. "He didn't leave nothing."

"Guess what?"

"What?"

"Cross your heart and hope to die?"

"Aw shit. Come on, Shrimp, stop the crap."

"You got to promise, though."

"Promise what?"

"You can't ever tell nobody. You swear? You promise?"

"For Christ sake, Linda!"

"Shhhh," she whispered fearfully. "I'm serious, Tony. Listen, you know Father Frank Jr.'s picture, the one used to be in the living room?"

"Yeah. It ain't there no more. That your news?"

"No. Pa told Ma she had to get it out of there, you know. Like it was a sacrilege, a sin or something, him sitting on the TV dressed up like a priest when he wasn't one no more. So, anyway, Ma took it off the TV and that was that. No one knew what she did with it, you understand. Then, when we come home from church, I see that Grandma isn't taking her coat off and I don't know why. Ma and Pa are in the kitchen. I think you was up here. Anyway, I go over to Grandma and try to help her take her coat off and she gives me like a wink, you know, and a 'shhh' and takes me over to the linen closet in the dining room and she tells me, signals me, you know, to keep an eye on the kitchen and she goes into the linen closet and comes out holding something under her coat and she takes my hand and we almost run upstairs."

"She got the picture of Frank Jr.?" Tony laughed.

"Yeah, yeah! Ain't she something." Linda smiled and shook her head in admiration. "They're maybe going to write him off, but not her. We got the picture stowed away in our room. You ever want to look at it, just tell me, okay."

Tony leaned over and kissed Linda's forehead.

"Hey, what'd you do that for?" she asked, pleased, glowing with sudden shyness. "You ain't never done that before, Tony. Wow."

"Disappear, hey," he ordered. Then he turned her around, slapped her butt and shoved her lightly in the direction of her room.

III

Monday

Monday was Monday—workday, payday, same as every other Monday—till Fusco said, "Hey, Tony, isn't that your father out there?"

Tony looked up from the cash register where he was ringing up a sale and looked over to the window where Fusco was pointing.

"Yeah," he said. "That's him."

His father was looking into the store. His hands were thrust deep into his jacket pockets and his shoulders were hunched forward. His posture read like a placard: Frank Manero, looking tough.

When Tony turned toward the window, his father lowered his head and appeared to be browsing.

"You going to see what he wants?" Fusco asked.

"Naw," Tony said. "I'm working. He wants something from me, he'll come in. My pa ain't exactly shy."

"Okay." Fusco shook his head. "It's your father, your business. You want to run out a minute, it's okay with me. You don't, it's also okay."

Tony walked toward the front of the store where a customer was wandering along one of the aisles. "Looking for a putty knife," the customer said, "like for fixing up where the putty's cracking around the tub. But I got to hurry. I'm working. I just ran out for five minutes to do this."

"Tub attached to the wall or standing free?" Tony asked. He wished the guy had wanted some paint, something that would necessitate using the ladder.

110

"It's like wall-to-wall up against the tiles. The back wall, the putty's all dried there and, like, chipping away. I got to put on new or patch it or something."

"Got something great. Cheaper and easier than if you tried to rip out the old stuff and start over. Comes in a tube, you don't even need a knife. And it's, like, plastic. Dries in an hour."

The man smiled gratefully. "Terrific. It's great to find someone knows their business these days. A little pride, you know. Most people, they just want to put in their time and leave. They couldn't care less."

Tony looked back to the window. His father was still out there. Again, when Tony looked up, Frank looked down.

"You know that guy out there?" the customer said, following Tony's gaze. "Poor old guy. Looks like he don't know what to do with himself, you know. Window-shopping in the middle of the day. He ought to be working. He wouldn't look so lost."

Tony turned away. He moved down the aisle quickly and got the plastic fill. "Over here," he called on his way to the cash register. He rang up the sale and waited for the customer to leave. When the man was out of sight, he walked outside.

"Hey," he said to his father.

Frank Sr. looked up, tried to pretend surprise, then gave it up. "Hey. So this is your place, huh?"

"Ain't exactly mine," Tony said.

"Big. Passed it lots of times, never noticed how big it was."

"Yeah. You all right? I mean, everything okay at home and all?"

"Oh sure, I was just taking a walk. Your mother, she's . . . cleaning and all that. You know. I just wanted to get the hell out of there."

"Oh," Tony said.

"All right. I was just walking. I'll see you home later. And don't be late. Your mother's got enough troubles without you being late all the time."

"Yeah, yeah. Right," Tony said. Then, without looking his father in the face; tentatively, quickly, he said, "I'm going on my lunch in about twenty minutes. You want to have some coffee? Some pizza or something?"

Frank's response was not so much predictable as inevitable. Although Tony had braced himself for it, he winced involuntarily. "What you crazy?!" Frank said, indignantly. "You think I ain't got nothing to do but hang out and go for pizza with you? Don't be late tonight, you hear me!"

"What did he want?" Fusco asked when Tony returned.

"Beats me," Tony said. "But nothing new."

Frank Sr. didn't explain at dinner that night either. In fact, he didn't mention his visit to Bayside Paints at all. When the women were clearing the table, he turned to Tony and said, "You pick up your big four bucks today?"

"Yeah," Tony said.

And Frank sneered. "Hot stuff. You really hot stuff, ain't you?"

Tony stared at him silently for a minute, then got up and left the table.

His immediate impulse was to get out of the house. But he went upstairs and showered and dressed and took his time. When he was ready to leave, Frank Sr. and Flo were watching TV. Linda was doing her homework in the dining room. He took his leather jacket down from the hook in the foyer and left without a word. He wanted to slam the door, but something told him that quiet was better.

On his way to the dance studio, he knew he was right. Quiet was better; holding-in was better. He could feel the energy he would have wasted on his father, on rushing, on running away. The frustration and anger was all balled-up inside him, now. And he had better things to do with all that extra steam.

Upstairs at Phillips, he walked past Pete straight to the back rooms. He slowed down in the corridor.

He walked very quietly and slowly, peering into one room after another cautiously yet casually.

Stephanie Mangano was in room six. She was doing exercises at the bar. There was no music on. She wasn't dancing. He stood in the doorway and just looked at her.

"Hi," she said warmly, when she saw him.

He didn't reply. He stood there staring at her peevishly, thrown by her apparent innocence of any wrongdoing.

"Why you standing out there?" she asked.

Suddenly it occurred to him that he probably looked, to her, the way his father had looked to him peering through the window of the paint store this afternoon. Woodenly, despite a conscious effort to appear more relaxed, he entered the practice studio.

"How come you weren't there Saturday?" he said.

"I didn't say I'd be there."

"Fuck you didn't."

"I said maybe. Maybe's maybe." She scrutinized his face. "I didn't think you'd get upset," she said honestly.

"Fuck that shit . . . upset. We're going to need all the practice we can, we going to win this thing."

"Okay," Stephanie said amiably. There was a faint smile on her lips. "Then let's practice."

"Didn't bring my albums. Didn't think you'd be here."

Her smile brightened with amusement. "Then why'd you come?"

"Hey, *stoogatz!*" he shouted angrily. "You know '*stoogatz?*' "

"I know '*stoogatz,*' " she said imitating his accent perfectly.

All of a sudden, he was grinning with her.

"Okay," he laughed. He crossed the room and turned the studio music on to the disco channel, then came halfway back and held his arms out to her.

"Okay," she said, moving into his arms. "Let's dance."

They warmed up quickly and rehearsed the routines they'd established. Then, they began trading off new ones again. He was watching her do some crisscross thing with her hands. He was counting the beat of the movement aloud.

"And one and cross and over and back. All right, nice. Where'd you get that one?"

"Come on, let's try it together," she said. "Got it, saw it, at a disco in the city," she explained as they worked the hand movements into a step.

"That where you were Saturday night? Dancing in beautiful, interesting Manhattan, with the beautiful, interesting people, at a beautiful, interesting disco?"

She laughed. "I'm moving next weekend. I told you I was going to—to beautiful, interesting Manhattan!"

"No kidding?" He was stung but impressed. Geographically, Manhattan was a spit away—easily accessible by tunnels, bridges, expressways, by a five minute subway ride. But, in every other way, Manhattan was separated from the rest of New York City by a distance, a difference, that went beyond mere time and space. Rules. Stephanie Mangano was moving to an alien world governed by different rules. She understood them and would be safe. He didn't.

"No kidding," she said joyously.

"Well, wow, that's great," he said halfheartedly. Suddenly, he stopped dancing. "Wait a minute. What about the Sweepstakes? You going to move the day of the Sweepstakes?"

"Well, I was going to talk to you about that. I was thinking that if I could maybe move most of the stuff one day during the week, I wouldn't have so much to do over the weekend. You know, I'd be fresher for the evening."

He was visibly relieved. "Sure. That makes sense. That's a good idea."

"Only thing, I don't have a car during the week. You know, everyone's working. My boss'll be out of town on Wednesday. I think I could get the day off. But no car."

"I got a friend with a Chevy," he said. "I'll check it out. It's all busted up and old but it's big. Maybe I could help out. You know, drive you over."

"Oh, Tony, that would be super!"

"Yeah, right. Super!" he said smiling grudgingly. "You think maybe we could work on a little dancing now? You think, maybe, that would be super?"

She laughed happily. "Sure," she said.

The rest of the session was almost more magical than the first time they'd danced together. There was less faltering, less self-consciousness, and more trust. That was the key to the way they moved. They moved as if they were mindless, communicating with their bodies alone. They moved as if their bodies trusted one another. For all the work and calculation that went into each series of steps, the reward was this seemingly effortless anticipation of who would be where at the end of a turn and precisely how the motion would melt into the next intricacy.

They stopped exhausted and pleased at the end of an hour and a half.

"We're going to take it," Tony said.

"We're good," Stephanie agreed.

They released each other with less self-consciousness, too, and they were still talking excitedly, appraising their progress, when they stepped through the door into the main studio.

"Visitors," Pete said sourly.

Beyond him, on a bench near the reception desk, the Faces sprawled carelessly.

"Hey," Tony called out in surprise.

Double J. ambled over. "Yeah. We been waiting. Pete said you was practicing." The pleasure on Tony's face as he'd come through the door troubled Double J. He looked from Tony to Stephanie trying to assess her contribution to it. She stared back at him without flinching. Double J. was not pleased.

"We was cruising the . . . you know who," Joey

coded crudely for Stephanie's benefit. "It's looking good for tonight," he told Tony.

"It's got to be later," Tony said. "We were just . . . Hey, I know, you guys don't know each other. This is Stephanie Mangano, my new dance partner," he said proudly. "Stephanie, that's Joey, Double J., and over there, that's Bobby C. I know him practically all my life. He's the one with the car I was telling you about."

Bobby C. waved from the bench. Stephanie smiled at him and said hello to the others.

Double J. ignored her. "Hey, what do you mean later? You known Bobby C. all your life—well, that's how Gus and me are, too, see. He helped me that time my old man was going to cut me up. They was both drunk as skunks, the old man and my ma. Wasn't for Gus getting me out of there, he would have sliced my fuckin face off. He's family to me, you understand? Some spic gives him a shove, I owe him!"

Tony stepped forward, away from Stephanie. "Double J.," he said softly. He put his arm around Double J.'s shoulder and walked him toward the desk. "What the fuck you laying out your whole life story for? Ain't Gus my friend, too? I said later, okay. I just worked my ass off. Let me go get a couple burgers, something, then we'll check it out, okay?"

"Yeah, yeah. Okay," Double J. said. "I'm edgy. I want some action, that's all. And what I said about Gus, that's the truth, too. You didn't see him over at the hospital."

"Come on," Tony said. He turned to the rest of them, "Come on. We'll go out, grab a pizza, a burger. It's early. We got time. Come on," he said to Stephanie. "We could drive you home, drop you off, right after we get something to eat. Okay?"

Stephanie glanced apprehensively at Double J.

"You from around here?" he asked.

She grinned delightedly. "Yeah," she said. "But just passing through."

"You was at 2001 a couple weeks ago," Joey said. "I thought I seen you somewhere."

"Great," Tony said. "Everyone knows everyone. Let's get out of here."

They decided on hamburgers. At the coffee shop, all five of them squeezed into a booth. Tony, Stephanie and little Bobby C. on one side, Double J. and Joey on the other. Tony would have preferred sharing the seat with Stephanie alone but Bobby C. didn't fit on the other side, and it wasn't really bad at all with Stephanie wedged between them.

Everyone was eating except Stephanie and Double J. He was making do with a coke and whatever french fries spilled to the table. Stephanie had her tea and lemon in front of her but, Tony noted with amusement, if she was waiting until the tea cooled, it would have been easier to order it iced.

"I may be traveling . . ." she was saying in her Manhattan dream voice, "promotional tours with authors and performers. Of course, I'll hate to leave the city even briefly—certain concerts, the ballet—"

Tony finished his first burger. He looked around the table at the Faces before reaching for the second one. He smiled to himself. Bobby C., Joey, and Double J. were listening to Stephanie, staring at her with the same mixture of awe and curiosity that he had felt the first time she'd talked to him.

"Hey, tell them about some of the people where you work," he prompted. Then he tore into the second hamburger.

"Well, you know who came in today! Elton John! He had on this sheepskin coat down to . . ."

"He's a faggot," Joey said decisively.

"A half-faggot," Double J. amended.

"I suppose you mean," Stephanie said superciliously, ". . . bisexual?"

"Yeah, swings both ways. Men and boys."

She glared at Double J., then her eyes narrowed with sudden cunning. "Oh, yeah," she continued breezily, "and Joe Namath was in. I brought him some coffee. He wanted me to have coffee with him and . . ."

The Faces snapped to respectful attention.

"You had coffee with Joe Namath!" Joey said.

"He wanted to know what being twenty-one was like. I told him I didn't know—I was twenty." She smiled and, finally, tasted her tea.

Tony looked around the table. He was smiling, almost benevolently, like a father proud of all his children for behaving exactly as he'd wished. The Faces were obviously impressed with Stephanie Mangano and she, in turn, seemed appropriately pleased with the audience he had provided for her. He picked up his third and last hamburger and began devouring it happily.

"Well, what else?" Double J. prodded Stephanie.

"That's all," she said.

"Ain't that enough?" Tony asked. His mouth was full. He laughed and choked and gulped the burger down, then laughed again and took another enormous bite.

"Jesus, you don't chew," Joey cautioned him. "I mean, hey Tony, you never chew."

"When my mother dies, I'll give you the job, okay?"

"You know what's going down your stomach?" Double J. said. "Big chunks, gobs of hamburger— like dog food, chunks, dog yummies, gobs of fat, friskies. You're going to turn into a dog, Tony, you know." Double J. started barking. Joey laughed and joined in. Then Bobby C. yelped and howled.

Suddenly, they were all barking and laughing and wildly excited. They began to leap up and snap ferociously at the waitress and other patrons. Joey jumped into the aisle and barked and snarled. Double J. growled at Joey and began swiping at him with a claw-like fist. Bobby C. jammed into a corner by Stephanie and Tony, finally, climbed over the back of the booth sending the couple at the next table scurrying, screaming, into the aisle.

"Hey, come on, you guys," Tony hollered. But he was laughing and the sound of his laughter only added to the noise and chaos.

Stephanie stared at them. Her face was a mask of horror and revulsion. She wanted to run, but dared not move. The Faces were blocking the aisle. All eyes were riveted on them. She flushed with embarrassment and rage and she sat very, very still until the manic seizure passed and all of them, except Tony, had scrambled out the door.

He took her arm and led her to the cashier's counter. She stared straight ahead, furious but, oddly enough, proud of her own performance. She didn't feel like crying or cringing anymore. She felt dignified, superior, triumphant. In some way, she was even grateful to the Faces for furnishing indisputable evidence of the gap that existed between her and them.

Bobby C.'s car was in front of the coffee shop when she and Tony came out. It took her only a moment to consider and accept the lift that had been offered to her. Tonight, the battered red Chevy would take her to her parents' house in Bay Ridge, Brooklyn. On Wednesday, it would transport her to her real home, her very own apartment, in Manhattan.

She got into the front seat with Tony and Bobby C. The car radio was on, and loud. She gave Bobby C. the directions, then sat back; glad that the music made conversation unnecessary, if not impossible. For the rest of the ride, she gave herself over to calculating how much she could cram into the car on Wednesday and which things she'd want or need first. When the car pulled up at the corner of the one-way street, she got out.

"Thanks," she said to Bobby C. and, to Tony: "See you." She turned to walk away but Bobby C. beckoned her back.

"Stephanie, something I gotta ask you," he said shyly, seriously. "If you were knocked up and you either had to get married or get an abortion, what would you do?"

"Who would I have to marry?" she asked.

"Me."

"I'd get an abortion." She waved to Tony and left.

Bobby C. sighed. "Now, why can't Pauline see it that way?" he said. He started up the car and looked at Tony. "Okay, where to?"

"You know where," Double J. called from the back seat.

"Barracudas' club house." Joey told him, "Right, Tony?"

"Yeah, let's do it," Tony said.

Bobby C. wheeled the car into a tight U-turn and, without enthusiasm, headed for the Spanish section of town. He shut off the radio, dimmed his lights and slowed the car two storefronts before the club house. Double J. jumped out and sauntered toward the Barracudas' headquarters. Bobby C.'s car followed just behind him. As he passed the club house, Double J. quickly glanced inside through a chink in the paint, then walked on. A few doors down the block, he moved to the curb and, when Joey threw the rear door open, he got back in and told Bobby C. to keep on going.

"They got a fucking army in there," he said. "Goddamn cucarachas!"

"Fuck it," Tony said. "I ain't in the mood anyway."

Bobby C. spun the car around the corner. "Yeah, me too," he agreed.

"Yeah?" Double J. growled. "Well, we going to do it sooner or later, man!"

"Ease up, Double J.," Joey said cautiously. "Gus is still in the hospital. We'll get them. We got time. We'll take one of them for every day he's laid up, okay?"

They drove in silence.

"Hey," Tony said after awhile, "what'd you think of her?"

"Who, Stephanie?"

"You really want to know," Double J. asked.

"Yeah."

"Snotty bitch."

"She's cool," Tony said. "You've got to get to know her, is all."

"You fuck her yet?" Joey asked.

Tony turned the radio on. He didn't answer.

Double J. leaned forward. He stared hard at Tony. He wasn't waiting for an answer, he was examining Tony's face as if he expected to see something in it, some change . . . something to justify the nervous feeling he had that Tony was pulling back, hanging somewhere between them and the girl.

"You fuck her?" Joey repeated.

"What do you think!" Tony shouted, finally.

Double J. sat back. "Keep seeing a chick who won't fuck you, you getting fucked, man," he said very softly. "Know what I mean?"

Tony started to turn, changed his mind and faced front sullenly. When the car was two blocks from his house, he told Bobby C. to let him out. He walked around to the driver's side.

"Almost forgot," he said. "Okay if I borrow the car Wednesday?"

"Sure. Where you going?" Bobby C. asked.

"Into the city . . . you know, Manhattan."

"What the hell you going to do in Manhattan?" Joey called from the back seat.

"I got business. Doing someone a favor, that's all."

"Who, the bionic woman?" Double J. laughed.

"See you," Tony said to Bobby C. and walked away.

"Pussy-whipped and no pussy. Jesus!" Double J. said, shaking his head and staring incredulously at Tony's retreating back.

Wednesday was sunny and clear and, according to the radio in the back room of Bayside Paints, the air quality for the day was expected to remain acceptable. Tony had gone into the back room looking for Dan Fusco. The store had been busy all morning, and he hadn't gotten a chance to talk to Fusco yet.

"Tony! Where are you?"

He hurried back out. Fusco was behind the cash register.

"What were you doing in the back? Look what's going on here," he waved at the scattering of customers wandering about the store.

"I was looking for you. Listen I got to talk to you a minute."

"First, them," Fusco said. "First talk to them, then me."

Tony waited on two customers. As he was ringing up the second sale, Fusco walked by. Tony shoved the change and the bag of plaster toward the man in front of the register, remembered to say thanks, then ran around the corner of the counter to intercept Fusco.

"Mr. Fusco, I've got to have the afternoon off," he said.

Fusco shook his head, no. "Sam's out. Harold's sick."

"I've got to, Mr. Fusco."

"Sorry, Tony."

"Hey, I would have told you yesterday only it was busy and I forgot. I got plans. Anyway, I been here almost eight months, didn't miss a day."

Fusco was getting annoyed. He lowered his voice as if he didn't want to be overheard. "Not today, Tony. You got it. Not today."

Tony looked around the store to see why Fusco was whispering. Only two customers and two employees were visible. Angrily, he pointed at the salesmen. "Some of them old farts, they're out three, four days at a time. You don't say nothing to them. All I'm asking for is half a day!"

"Cool off, Tony."

"Well, I've got to have it—and I'm taking it."

"You do that," Fusco warned, "and you're fired."

"I'm doing it!" Tony shouted.

"Then you're fired."

Tony glared at him, turned and stalked into the back room. A minute later, he reappeared carrying his leather jacket. He didn't look at Fusco. He glanced

up at the wall clock. It was a little after eleven.
"Great," he said. "I got an extra hour and a half.
Just goddamned terrific!" and he stormed past Fus-
co out of the store.

He kept on going till he got to the pizza parlor.
His anger had subsided and he felt a bit dazed. The
counterman was leaning on his elbows looking out
the window. Tony held three fingers up to him and
walked inside.

"Lemme have a coke, too," he called as he
headed for the pay phone on the back wall. He
dialed the stereo store and asked for the repair department. They put him on hold. Finally, someone
picked up and said "Yeah?" impatiently.

"Bobby there?" he asked.

"Bobby who?"

"Bobby C.," Tony said, "This is . . . I'm a friend
of the family. His mother gave me this number for
an emergency."

"This an emergency?" the man asked, less gruff-
ly.

"Yeah, but don't say anything to him. I don't
want to shock him or anything."

Bobby C. got on the line. "I'm fired," Tony said.
"You shocked?"

"Yeah." Bobby C. breathed. "Jesus, what happened?"

"Just stay shocked . . . look upset, okay. Is that
guy who answered watching you?"

"Uh, yeah." Bobby C. sounded confused.

"I told him it was an emergency. I'm at the pizza
parlor. Can you get out early, meet me?"

There was a warning click on the phone. The
next interruption would be the recorded reminder to
deposit more money.

"Can you meet me?" Tony repeated.

"Right," Bobby C. said. "I'll be right there."

Tony took a seat at the counter. He drank the
coke. When the pizza was ready, he piled the slices
one on top of another and took an enormous bite.
Just as he finished the triple-decker, Bobby C. came

running into the pizza parlor. He practically skidded to a halt, then leaned back against the stool next to Tony's to catch his breath.

"What'd you tell them?" Tony asked.

"Nothing. I just hung up and ran out."

"No kidding? That's wild. Why'd you do that?"

"What I got to lose?" Bobby C. asked forlornly.

Tony burst out laughing.

Bobby C. looked up at him, grinned mournfully and shrugged. "I couldn't think of an emergency," he said. "Anyway, what are they going to do? The best thing could happen to me right now's if they canned me. If I didn't have a job, maybe Pauline's parents, they'd see I was no good."

"You jerk-off." Tony was still laughing. "All you been talking for a month now is Pauline being pregnant. You been telling the whole world. You go back to work, they'll probably have cigars waiting for you. Think you ran over to the maternity ward to see your kid, or something."

"Hey, what about you?" Bobby C. asked suddenly. "You really get fired?"

"Yeah." Tony slid some change across the counter and hopped off the stool. "Come on, let's walk over to the car. Where'd you park it? You bring the keys?"

They walked out onto 86th Street.

"I'm over near Fourth, a couple of blocks. I got the keys right here. Well, come on, what happened? I thought you just got a raise. How come you're fired?"

"He didn't want to let me have the afternoon off. I got pissed. Don't matter."

"'Cause you had to go to Manhattan? You walked off of a job 'cause you had to do someone a favor?"

"Yeah," Tony said. "I told you, it don't matter."

"What's the favor?" Bobby C. asked fearfully. "What's so important? You in some kind of trouble?"

"Shit, no. I'm helping Stephanie move. She just got an apartment in the city. She's supposed to move in on Saturday and Saturday night's the Sweepstakes at 2001. She's my partner."

Bobby C. considered for a while. "It's a fucking riot," he said somberly. "You're willing to blow your job for a chick you ain't even balled yet—and me—oh my fucking Christ almighty, what am I going to do?! Tony, I don't want to marry her!"

They turned the corner. On the side street, Bobby C. lowered his voice but his tone became more urgent. He began to gesture wildly with his hands; he prayed, he punched the air, he pulled at his collar like a strangling man.

"I don't want to marry her. I don't give a shit about her. I can't stand the ugly bitch."

"Then don't marry her," Tony said.

"I gotta—she won't have an abortion. Everybody says I gotta."

"Who?"

"Her fucking parents. My parents. The fucking priest. Even her fucking high school guidance counselor."

The Chevy was about fifty feet away, parked between two driveways on the treeless residential street. Bobby C. stopped suddenly.

"Tony, it's got me like . . . paralyzed," he whispered. "Like I don't got no control over my life. Tony, we always been like best friends, a lot alike—how come I'm fucking up and you're okay?"

"Who's okay?" Tony said. Then, rubbing Bobby C.'s curly head, he tried to smile. "Aw, shit, you just got to hang in. Maybe it'll work out."

They walked to the car. Bobby C. looking wretched, looking on the verge of tears, nodded his head in response to Tony's advice. He reached into his pocket and handed over the car keys.

"Hang in there," Tony told him again. He got into the car, waved to Bobby C., and took off for Stephanie's house.

When he drove up, she was waiting. She was sitting on the steps reading a book, surrounded by tidy cartons and a few larger household items. She jumped up when she saw him, grabbed the nearest item—a lamp—and ran to the car.

"You look like the Statue of Liberty," he said.

She looked at the lamp and the book in her hand and started to laugh. "I am . . . almost." She opened the rear door and laid the lamp down. She threw the book onto the front seat and ran back to the steps. Tony was carrying two of the cartons and a mirror to the car. Stephanie took the ironing board. They'd packed just about everything in five minutes. Stephanie got into the car and closed her door while Tony put the last carton in the trunk.

She was combing her hair when he got behind the wheel.

"Aren't you going to say goodbye to anyone?" he asked.

Stephanie looked at the house and wrinkled her nose.

"Nobody home?" Tony said. He started the car and pulled away.

"You might say that," she laughed. "There's been nobody home in that house for as long as I can remember. Goodbye," she called out with sudden exuberance. "Goodbye! Goodbye! Shit! I'm coming back tonight, aren't I?"

"Oh yeah, I almost forgot."

She turned the radio on and they drove without speaking for awhile.

"This got me fired," Tony said suddenly.

"You got fired?"

"Yeah," he said. His voice was surly. "You couldn't move this stuff on Sunday?"

"I . . . I just wanted to get everything in—so I could start fixing it up over the weekend." She looked over at him. "Why'd you get fired?"

"Forget it," he said.

"Because of moving me?"

He didn't answer.

"I got the day off. Nobody bitched at my office," she said defensively. Then after a pause, she added, "I'm sorry."

"Forget it, I said."

He turned the radio up. She looked out her window. The Expressway was only moderately crowded. They made good time. When the Manhattan skyline came into view, he could almost feel her excitement, practically see her straining at the window like a kid outside a candy store. It annoyed him. He was glad when the car entered the tunnel and there was nothing for her to look at but the grimy yellow tiles or him.

On the other side of the tunnel, she gave him directions to her apartment. They drove uptown on the East side and she pointed out restaurants and bars she'd been to and boutiques and where Bloomingdale's was. Her office was a few blocks west of the one-way avenue they were on. At 72nd Street, she told him to turn left and they drove along a wide two-way street that narrowed into a roadway through Central Park. As they emerged from the park, she pointed out a huge brown building that looked like an armory.

"That's the Dakota," she told him. "Where *Rosemary's Baby* took place. And John and Yoko live there. I'm just two blocks away, on 74th."

The Dakota—weird, he thought: the streets were numbered, the buildings had names. "Who lives on your block, the Exorcist?"

"Very funny," she said. Then she laughed.

"Hey," he reminded her. "You're one of those people who says 'very funny,' you ain't supposed to laugh, remember."

"I'm happy! I can't help laughing!"

He pulled up in front of a narrow brownstone on West 74th Street. She got out of the car and fished around in her purse for the keys. Tony inspected the street casually. It was neat and tree-lined. Most of the buildings were old—renovated brownstones, five, six stories high. Almost every window on the block was stuffed with plants—real ones—in clay or glazed ceramic pots on sills or shelves or hanging in woven straw baskets.

He opened the trunk and took out two cartons.

Stephanie had gotten the lamp and a small shopping bag from the back seat. She was waiting for him at the door to the building.

"Well?" she said.

"Well, what?"

"How do you like it?"

"What, the street? It's okay. It ain't Bay Ridge, if that's what you mean."

She beamed at him. "Wait'll you see the inside. It's got all this incredible wood trim. Oak and real old, you know. It's all renovated. Stripped down to the original woodwork."

He followed her in and up the stairs which were narrow and carpeted. The bannister was dark wood, polished to a smooth, shiny finish. She stopped in front of an ordinary looking door and set the lamp down. She unlatched one lock easily. The second appeared to be open. He saw a flash of apprehension cross her face, then she picked up the lamp and nudged the door open with her knee and he followed her inside.

He had expected a bare apartment. The room, L-shaped and airy with an ornate fireplace set in one wall, was sparsely but handsomely furnished. There were even plants on the window sill. Stephanie appeared to be puzzled by the furniture, too. But, with loving familiarity, she ran her hand across the back of a Victorian sofa and said nothing.

Tony set the cartons down near the fireplace. Before he could comment on the apartment or its furnishings, a man dressed in jeans and a red-checked shirt came out of the kitchen. He was carrying an opened can of beer. He was smiling, attractive but a bit paunchy, and too old for jeans—even jeans that had obviously been dry-cleaned.

His smile warm, hearty, just a touch of amusement in it, acknowledged Stephanie's presence and her surprise at seeing him. Actually, she seemed upset to see him, unprepared and oddly flustered. But there was no doubt that she knew him.

Tony was stunned.

"I thought you were out of town," Stephanie said. The carefully cultivated sophistication was gone from her voice. She sounded very much the way she looked, particularly compared to the man. She sounded uneasy and almost childishly young.

The man walked over to her and put his arms behind her back. "I postponed the trip," he said, drawing her forward into a familiar embrace. She seemed to hesitate for a moment then, with some inner resistance still apparent, she moved toward him. He lifted her face and kissed her. First, she merely accepted his lips. Then with sudden emotion, she kissed him back.

Tony stood beside the fireplace staring at them. His hand was resting on the mantelpiece and the tension within him was so great that he had to press his palm hard and flat against the cold marble surface to stop it from shaking . . . to stop it from curling into a fist. Shock and rage riveted him—goading and paralyzing him at once. Just when he felt he would snap, Stephanie and the man separated. He saw Stephanie's eyes. They were filled with a hurt and tenderness that appalled him.

"Jay," Stephanie said, releasing the man's hand, "this is Tony Manero, a friend. Tony, Jay Langhart."

Jay laughed. "Unspecified status," he noted, then turned to Tony. "How do you do?"

Tony tried hard. He could not smile. "Pleased to meet you," he said and he didn't give a damn that it came out sounding like a recorded announcement.

Jay didn't seem concerned, either. "Listen," he said to Stephanie, "I've decided to leave you all the furniture."

"Super!"

"Stephanie," Langhart said with a patient smile, "nobody says 'super' anymore."

Stephanie lowered her head. She looked like a child who'd just been spanked. Tony had never seen her so chastened. It was amazing to him how easily the man could humble her, put her down with a single sentence and a sugary smile.

"You're not taking anything?" Stephanie asked.

"I'm going to start fresh in the new place," Jay said. Then, with offhanded magnanimity, he added, "What the hell, you picked out most of the stuff here, anyway."

Tony turned to Stephanie as if seeking confirmation of the extraordinary statement. Her eyes were on Jay. Her eyes were wide and puppy-dog eager.

"I . . . I read the book you told me to," she said.

"Kerr or Lawson?"

"Kerr." She smiled proudly.

"You didn't read Lawson?" Jay said. It wasn't so much a question as a sharp reproach, tempered, very slightly, by disappointment.

Stephanie was crushed again. "No," she confessed in a whisper.

Tony had heard enough and seen too much. "I'll get the rest of the stuff," he said. Without glancing at either of them again, he rushed out of the apartment.

Downstairs, he lit a cigarette, took a few puffs and tossed it away. Then he began unloading the car. He stacked the cartons on the sidewalk. Most of the boxes appeared to be filled with clothing or linens or articles so excellently wrapped that they made only a dull thud when they hit the street. The sound of utensils clattering or crockery crashing dangerously inside the cartons gave him no satisfaction. Nothing did. Still the sheer physical energy expended on lifting and setting the boxes down began to ease his tension a little bit.

Stephanie called to him from the window. "Please wait. I'll be right down."

He lit another cigarette.

She looked ready to cry as she came out into the street. She was terribly nervous. "I . . . one of us should stay down here . . . to watch the boxes. Somebody might . . . people take things if you leave them out."

"Sounds like a terrific block, really high class."

"Jay said one of us should probably keep an eye out, at least until everything is inside."

"You pretty used to doing what Jay says."

Her eyes registered the rebuke. "He knows the neighborhood," she said softly.

"Sure. And you use a Seeing Eye dog when you come to visit him."

"Please, Tony. Not now," she pleaded. "I . . . really, I just want to get the stuff upstairs and go. I didn't know he was going to be here, so help me. You know that. You saw it. You know I didn't expect anything like this."

"*You* didn't expect! Shit!"

She piled two cartons up, carried them into the brownstone and came back out. Without a word, he took the last of the boxes into the building. He left them in the hallway, at the foot of the stairs, alongside the cartons she'd set down there. When he walked back out, she had gathered up the ironing board, a blender, and a few large books. There was nothing else. He watched her go inside, then he got into the car and waited.

She returned sooner than he'd expected. She got into the car and closed the door and stared straight ahead. She didn't look up at the apartment window or over at him. He watched her, glared at her furiously for a minute, then started the car and pulled away from the curb. He drove fast, recklessly. He jumped a traffic light and left a squeal of brakes and a chorus of angry horns and curses in his wake before he slowed down.

Stephanie said nothing.

Finally, as they pulled away from the toll booths east of the Midtown Tunnel, as Manhattan became only the direction in which the car's exhaust fumes were aimed, Tony said: "What's he to you?"

She had been anticipating an explosion, not a question. She had waited, feeling exhausted and defenseless. Now, emotionally drained but relieved, she told him the truth.

"He's an arranger, a record producer. He wants

to do films. I met him at the agency. He's moving into a better apartment—more expensive—now that
his divorce is final. He didn't want his wife to know
how much money he had." She hesitated. "I lived
with him for awhile."

"Shit," he said.

"He taught me things. I learned a lot from
him."

"He sure knows how to put you down fast." He
was seething, glowering at her, but he felt curiously
relieved, too. "He your first guy?"

"No."

It caught him off guard. "No?"

"No."

"He your last guy?"

"No."

Tony looked at her suspiciously. He thought
about how often she'd exaggerated, maybe even lied
to him, in the past. "No?!" he said, half expecting to
see a teasing smile on her face; half hoping she was
lying to him now.

She was perfectly serious. "No," she repeated.

"Shit. Who else?"

"You want a list?"

"No," he shouted.

He drove silently for a little while, trying to regain his composure. His lack of control irked him.
When he felt cooler, he said, "What happened—I
mean, you and him?"

He was surprised and annoyed that there was
still anger in his voice.

"He got bored with me, I guess," Stephanie said
calmly. Then, "Shit! But he's still fond of me, he still
likes me."

Tony heard the anguish seep into her words,
heard her breaking down, at last. Uncontrollably, he
attacked.

"Likes to have you around for a quick piece
now and then—when he feels like it, right?" he said
savagely.

She burst into tears. She covered her face with

her hands and began to sob. Her shoulders shook, her whole body heaved convulsively. Torn between sympathy and the remnants of his own outrage, he watched her. The expression on his face remained harsh and contemptuous.

"He helped me," she wailed suddenly.

"Helped you in and out of the sack . . . the fucking old . . ."

"You don't know what working in a place like that is," she sobbed, "the agency. It's scary. There's so much you don't know. He . . . he built up my confidence, told me I could do it." She was hiccuping back the tears. "People there, they all went to college. And they've got . . . style . . . like the kind you don't just pick up overnight. They talk. They talk about things I never heard of—theater, politics, history. I feel so out of it, so dumb sometimes. If I said 'I don't know' every time I didn't know something . . . when I get asked to do something . . . I'd be saying 'I don't know' ten times a minute. So I just smile and fake something. I hope I learn how to do it. Figure it out later."

She stopped, gasping for breath. Finally, she took a long calming swallow. She sniffled once, loudly, and wound down with a tremendous shudder. "It kills you," she said. "You feel so scared and stupid."

Tony stared at her. She looked small and vulnerable. Her eyes were wide and wet and imploring him to understand. He was astonished.

He turned onto Shore Road and found a place to park. Stephanie was still crying. He got out of the car and walked around to her side.

"Come on. It's pretty here, nice. It's a good place to walk."

She got out and followed him down into the park. The bridge was aflame with late afternoon sunlight. They walked toward it along the water's edge.

"I haven't cried with anyone for two months," she said.

"Where you been doing your crying?"

She looked to see if he was serious. Then she

laughed. Her eyes were still red and glistening tears clung to her lashes, but she looked at him and laughed aloud and shook her head in amazement.

They walked along silently for a while. Each of them, instinctively, offering and accepting from the other a necessary distance—the time and space to sort through the turmoil of the afternoon's events; to remember, evaluate, even to forget. It was chilly near the water. It was easy to slip back into the grip of melancholy again. When Tony spoke, there was a trace of bitterness left.

"How come he couldn't help you move?"

Stephanie shrugged. "He doesn't have a car."

"He could have rented one. I don't like it. I don't like how he . . . . Why do you let him . . . Aw, shit! Could you win a dance contest with that old fuck?"

"Please, Tony," she said.

He bent down and pulled a fist full of wintry straw grass from the earth. A clod of soil came up with it. He walked toward the water and flung the muddy ball in the direction of the Verrazano Narrows Bridge.

"You know how tall that bridge is?" he called to Stephanie.

She turned toward the shimmering arch and shook her head.

"The towers go up 690 feet. Center span is 228 feet. They got forty million cars going across it a year. They got 127,000 tons of steel, almost three quarter million cubic yards of concrete. Center span is 4,260 feet—total length including approach ramps—over two and a half miles."

She walked over to him, smiling.

"You know all that!"

"Sure," he said. "I know everything about it. They've even got a guy buried in the concrete. He fell into it when they were building the bridge. Sometimes—after 2001, on a Saturday night, you know—we drive up there, me and Bobby C. and the other guys. We swing from the cables. I don't know, we almost fly. Sounds dumb, don't it?"

Stephanie looked up at the bridge, trying to imagine what he had just described. She hugged her coat more tightly around her. "Sounds dangerous."

"I come down here a lot, too. Look at it. Get ideas."

"What kind of ideas?"

"You know, ideas. Daydreams like. I don't know how to explain. When you talk about Manhattan, you sound a certain way. Not the bullshit, the other. It reminds me of when I come down here . . ."

She looked at him curiously. There was a raw beauty in his face. Just now, caught in the crisp chill of evening, in the setting sun's glow, staring off at the bridge . . . There was something about him—different, special, something.

He was handsome, of course, by Bay Ridge standards. He was the tall, dark, cool one that every high school girl wanted to own. In Manhattan, the same looks belonged to every other delivery boy; the kid in the stock room, an elevator operator's nephew, the doorman's son.

How silly, she thought suddenly. It wasn't that Tony had changed. It was only that she could not imagine that Jay Langhart's weathered face had ever looked that young or innocent or yearning.

"I'm cold," she said. "Let's go."

They drove back to her house. Tony parked Bobby C.'s car in front of the sidewalk, in front of the steps on which she'd been waiting for him so many hours ago. There were lights on in her house now and she was looking at them. Her hand was on the door handle, her back to him. Finally, she opened the door and began to get out. Then, impulsively, she turned and leaned over and kissed him quickly on the cheek.

"Thanks," she said.

He grabbed her arm and pulled her closer. He felt her stiffen with resistance but he expected that to subside so he continued to hold her while she tried to pull back, pull away from him. He put both arms around her and tried to kiss her. She twisted her head away. Angry and confused, he released her. He shoved her toward the door, then grasped her wrist.

"Goddamit!" he shouted. "How come you won't make it with me?"

She glared at him, glared at the hand that was squeezing her wrist. "I told you once. For me to go to bed with you would be a step backward."

"So take a step backward. Then take a step forward. Ain't that what they call progress?"

He felt her hand relax in his grasp.

"Tony, I'm also into being . . . imitating . . . a nice girl these days." He felt her open his hand, the hand in which hers was caught. He let her open it finger by finger. He watched her rub her bruised wrist. He didn't look at her face.

"What are you?" he said. "What the fuck are you? You're not a nice girl . . . and you're not a cunt exactly. . . ."

"How about, maybe . . . a person? A friend?"

He looked up at her. She was serious. Then she started to smile. She smiled at him and blew him a kiss and scooted out of the car before he really understood what she'd said.

"The way we feel when we dance . . ." he called out after her, "that ain't friends."

It didn't matter. She hadn't heard him. She'd gone —up the sidewalk and the steps and across the porch and pulled the storm door shut behind her.

He sat in the car for a few minutes more. He tore at a hangnail on his finger, then bit it absently, then finally spit it out and started the motor and drove off.

Bobby C.'s house was less than five minutes away. Tony pulled the car into the Corelli's driveway and walked around to the back door of the tiny two-family house. It looked like every other one on the block, dilapidated but decorated. Two stories high and it didn't matter if the roof leaked or the siding was rusting through the paint, there was a rose bush or a cement virgin or a one-legged flamingo pecking at the four square feet of crab grass out front.

Mr. Corelli answered the door. He filled the door

with his stocky frame. Tony could see Bobby C. behind his father motioning frantically, clasping his
palms in an anguished imitation of prayer. There was
a priest visible, too, which undoubtedly accounted
for the fact that Corelli was wearing a regular shirt.

"Just came to return the car keys," Tony said.

Corelli grunted. "Good." He took the keys from
Tony and shut the door.

He made it back home in time for dinner. He
ate quickly and went up to his room and it wasn't till
he was up there listening to Paulie's album that he
remembered he'd been fired and that he hadn't said
anything about it.

The next morning he woke, without the alarm
clock going off, at his usual workday time. He shook
his head and put his feet on the floor and rubbed his
eyes and stretched. He showered and shaved and
deodorized and cologned and dressed and blew dry
and knew, all of a sudden, that he was going to leave
the house as if nothing had happened.

He walked over to 86th Street and stopped at the
luncheonette. Not having a job, a destination, a sched-
ule, felt funny. He wondered if it would change him
as it was changing his father. Somewhere in the
back of his mind, he thought he should start worrying. But, this morning, he felt free, lightheaded, almost rich. He went inside and took a stool at the
counter and studied the breakfast menu.

He glanced over the numbered specials: the 79¢
coffee-egg-toast combination; the $1.79 for one more
egg, juice and bacon. He passed up the #5 French
toast combo and the more expensive hot cakes de-
luxe. When he finally ordered, he ordered lavishly
and none of the specials. He ordered large juice, two
fried eggs on a stack of pancakes, bacon, ham *and*
sausage, a side of home fries, a coke and coffee. He
ordered defiantly. He ate everything. He tasted nothing. He paid gladly and left a dollar tip. Then he decided to stop in at Bayside Paints to pick up the
last of his salary.

Fusco was in the utility room poring over a book-keeping ledger. Tony tapped him on shoulder and said, quietly so the old man wouldn't jump out of his skin, "I came for what I got coming."

Fusco turned to him and smiled.

"Tony, Tony . . . Hey!"

"Hi, ya," Tony said. "I . . . uh. I figure you owe me a couple of days—and a half."

"Things, they got a little hot under the collar, don't you think?" Fusco said.

"What?"

Fusco stood and put his arm around Tony's shoulder. "I don't want to lose you, Tony. You're a smart kid. Customers like you. I want you to stay on."

"You mean I'm not fired?"

"No," Fusco said.

"Well, Jesus Christ!" Tony beamed. He took his leather jacket off and tossed it onto the wall peg. Fusco smiled at him benevolently and they walked out of the utility room together.

"You got a future here, Tony." He was changing into his salesman's jacket when Fusco pointed to the floor men. "Sam, over there," he said. "Been here eighteen years. Mike—fifteen years."

"Excuse me, Mr. Fusco," Tony said quickly, cutting him off. "I got to go to the john a minute."

"Sure, sure."

Tony turned and headed for the back of the store again. He'd felt so good when Fusco rehired him; good and grateful, too. But, eighteen years? Fifteen years? Shit! He was glad he'd had that breakfast. The goddamn pancakes were dancing with the sausages in his belly but, at least, he consoled himself as he hurried toward the bathroom, he'd have something real to throw up.

He got through the day. Lunchtime, he went over to the stereo shop, but Bobby C. wasn't there. The foreman in the basement hole that was the repair department told him that Bobby'd been acting strange.

"Weird," was what the man said. "Yesterday, he run out a here for a fuckin' phone call. Didn't tell nobody how come. Left parts laying all the hell around where he was working. He come back, of course. But wouldn't say shit where he was. I almost told him to get his ass out. If I could of put the machine he took apart together, I would of, too. Today, like the same thing. He's working, then he's gone. No phone call even. He's been moping around, looking like a zombie for about a week and now he's cutting out whenever he feels like it. You his friend? Give him some friendly advice. Tell him to shape up!"

On his way back to Bayside Paints, he saw Bobby C. running toward him.

"Hey, I was just over your store, looking for you," Tony said.

Bobby C. slowed down. "I'm late. I getta get back to the shop," he blurted out. "Tony, I'm dying, I swear to you." Then he ran on.

Fusco fawned over him most of the afternoon.

Winking, smiling, giving him those atta-boy looks every time he passed—he didn't mind that. But, by closing time, Fusco had told six different customers Tony was waiting on how they really ought to see the kid ride that ladder and how fast Tony could find anything in the store and how much money he had saved professional painters with his knowledgeable advice.

By closing time, Tony was almost grateful to be going home where he could count on someone to find something to bitch at him about.

IV

Thursday Night

There were only two evenings left to rehearse. All through dinner he was conscious of that. He couldn't concentrate on anything else. As he ate, he reviewed the steps he and Stephanie already had down; the ones they'd have to work on tonight and polish perfectly tomorrow. He considered which records he should bring to the studio. Maybe some that they hadn't danced to yet. You couldn't tell what Bernie might choose to play for the Sweepstakes.

His father punched his arm. "Hey, you gonna pass your mother that plate or you figure the whole damn chicken's for you?"

"What?"

"I said pass your mother the chicken, that's what!"

Tony passed the platter.

He wished he had at least one Latin disco album in his collection—just in case. But they were going to win anyway. He was good, Stephanie was good; and no one had seen them dance together yet! Except Pete, just once, and that was their very first time. They were going to win dancing, that part was easy. But they were going to take it with style, class . . . and that, he knew, he couldn't have without her.

"Hey! You lookin to make the Olympics?" his father said.

"What?"

"First off, you're eating like this is your first and last meal. You don't hear nothing. You ain't said one

140

word since you sat down. And you're helping yourself to thirds before your sister gets a chance to finish one lousy chicken leg."

"M'sorry," he said to Linda. She smiled and shrugged. Tony left the table and went upstairs to dress and pick out the records for the night.

Nobody was in the main room of the dance studio. Tony went into the back area. There was disco music coming from one of the practice rooms. He shuffled through the albums he'd brought with him as he walked down the corridor toward the music. The door was open.

He was rearranging the order of the albums when he got to the room. His head was down. He said, "Hi," before he looked up, called it out from the doorway before he realized that Stephanie was not alone in the room. She hadn't heard him. Neither had Pete who was dancing with her. They were doing the hustle. And talking. And laughing.

Tony stood still in the doorway. It was like watching her with that old man again. It was worse. Jay and his immaculate jeans and hearty good manners were a world away; not just in distance, but time. Jay was something from the past, in the past. It was over between them, she'd said.

Pete was now . . . now that she knew Tony, now that she was his partner! Pete was neighborhood, two steps backward; local and so low that even Annette had shuddered with disgust when she met him.

Tony whirled around, ready to rush out. He took a few steps, stopped, then turned and entered the practice room. Pete saw him first and started to smile.

"Trying to get it up to seventy per cent?" Tony said, impaling them both with his eyes. His face was deadly grim, his voice menacing.

The smile froze on Pete's lips and melted to a look of genuine surprise.

"Didn't know you hung your label on her," he said. He stared at Tony for a moment, hurt and bewildered. Then he drew himself up pridefully and stalked out.

Stephanie waited. She watched Tony silently.

"You know that guy?" he said. "That fuckin worm is the cocksman of Bay Ridge."

"My God—" she said icily. "I've been in serious danger."

"It's no fucking joke."

"God, you can be a fool," she said. She walked to the wall panel and lowered the music.

"Goddam right, I can be a fool," Tony shouted. "I've been a fool, thinking I could be the dance partner of a . . ."

"Gee, Tony, all the nasty, dirty words you know. You mean you can't think of one now?"

He turned and ran out of the room. In the corridor he collided with a short, slender boy wearing tights and a kimono-like jacket. As he reached out to regain his balance, the records flew out of his hands.

"Faggot," he spat at the boy.

The boy had knelt to help him gather the records. He stood abruptly, winged one album down the hallway and faced Tony with a defiant smile.

"Don't mess with him!" Pete called from the other end of the corridor.

The alarm in Pete's voice held Tony long enough for him to notice the belt of the boy's kimono— brown or black, he wasn't sure. Then Pete was charging toward them shouting, "Not in here, you don't. Cool out, Tony. Shelley, none of your fuckin Bruce Lee shit!"

"The . . . whaddya call it, those stockings . . ." Tony pointed to the tights. "I . . . sorry, man. Didn't know you were into martial arts."

"Tony Manero," Pete stood between them. "This is Sheldon Marx. He works out here sometimes. A champeen brown belt, ain't you, Shelley? Uh, Tony, Shelley gets real excited, real fast."

Tony noticed that Peter had taken hold of the boy's arm and was grasping it firmly. He bent and picked up his albums, all except the one Sheldon Marx had flung down the corridor.

"He knows he ain't supposed to pull no shit here," Pete continued. "But sometimes Shelley forgets I'm doing him a favor. Uh, whyn't you get your records and split now, okay?"

"Yeah, okay," Tony said. Then to the boy, "So you're a regular Bruce Lee . . ."

"Nothing regular about him." Pete laughed weakly.

"*Miss* Lee to you, sucker!" Sheldon hissed.

"He's a faggot!"

"Cool it, Tony," Pete shouted and dragged the recalcitrant brown belt into the nearest practice room.

"A faggot! A fucking champion brown belt cocksucker faggot!" Tony roared.

A fag, a cunt hound, and a cheating bitch—he'd like to kill them all! He grabbed the last album and ran out. He took the stairs two, three at a time and kicked the street door open and was still frustrated and furious when Annette came running toward him excitedly, shouting his name. He kept on going and she became frantic.

"Tony! Tony! Wait! Look!" she shouted breathlessly.

Finally, he slowed down and she trotted beside him fumbling in her purse. He stopped, waited. Her search became more agitated.

"I got them!" she said, at last; and triumphantly pulled a package of prophylactics out of her purse and dangled it in front of him.

"Oh, shit," he said, and rushed away leaving her waving a goddamned package of scumbags under the street lamp.

Bobby C.'s Chevy cut him off at the next corner. Joey leaned out the back window.

"We was just coming to get you. It's prime, tonight, Tony. *Primo* in cucaracha land!"

Tony got into the front seat. "Great," he said. "Let's go."

"Y'see that," Joey said. "I told you he'd make it, didn't I? You got no faith, Double J."

"Fuck off, Joey, huh."

"Your problem's you don't trust no one; you wouldn't trust your own mother."

"You knew my mother, asshole, you'd know how funny you are!"

"Something wrong, Double J?" Tony said.

"Naw."

"He didn't think you'd go along with it. Thinks you're pulling away from the guys 'cause a . . . you know, that chick."

"Hey, Joey, I told you, fuck off!"

Tony glanced at Bobby C. who hadn't spoken since he'd gotten into the car. Bobby C. was staring straight ahead, driving, but with that crazy, dazed look that said no one was really behind the wheel.

"You okay?" Tony asked.

Bobby C. nodded. His eyes were wildly unfocused. He moved his lips as if he were going to speak. Some small sounds emerged, low, birdlike. Then his lips didn't so much close as settle down and he was utterly silent again.

"A'right," Double J. said. "Turn and lower the lights."

They were on the Barracudas' turf. They followed the exploration procedure established on the previous runs. Bobby C. slowed just before the club house. Double J. got out, kept pace with the car, peered into the storefront, walked on and got back into the car a few doors down the block from the Barracudas' headquarters. Then, Bobby C. picked up speed and turned the corner.

This time, Double J. was smiling.

"Okay," he said.

"Six?" Joey asked. There was a touch of apprehension in his voice. He tried to pass it off as excitement. "Same six as before?!"

"Four," Double J. answered, savouring the word. "Fucking four. It's beautiful. They got four Barracudas; yeah, and two girls in there."

"That's six," Bobby C. said. "Could wait awhile ... get down to three, four...."

"Or one or two," Joey said contemptuously.

"Ain't six," Double J. asserted. "There were six before. Now there's four, you understand! Four little bitty greasers and two girls. We lost two fucking guys just by going for Tony. Could have had us six for the same price. Now there's just four!"

"Go on, drive around again," Joey ordered. "Come in on them quiet."

"Tony?" Double J. asked.

"Go," he said.

Bobby C. was driving. "Tony!" he wailed suddenly, "Pauline . . . her parents, my parents, they set the fucking date!"

Tony stared at him; his eyes flashed angrily, then he shook his head in disgust.

"What've we got?" he asked.

"Me and Double J. got blades," Joey said. "There's a chain back here, if you want it. Fat, but it'd go 'round your fist, maybe. And a baseball bat, would you believe."

"I ain't got no knife. I ain't got shit," Bobby C. said.

"Here." Tony reached down and pulled an empty beer bottle from the floor.

"Great," Bobby C. said. "What the fuck I do with that—piss in it or collect blood?"

Tony put his arm out the car window and slammed the bottom of the bottle against the door. It broke cleanly. He handed the razor-edged neck to Bobby C.

"Collect blood," he said. "Gimme the bat and the chain, or any other bottle you got back there."

"You're in luck," Joey laughed. "You got a choice —beer or vodka?"

"Just break one."

"Okay, can the shit and back up!" Double J. said.

"What?" Bobby C. said.

Double J. scrambled over into the front seat. They had passed the club house. "Back up!" he ordered.

Bobby C. threw the car into reverse.

"Okay. Forward. Now!"

Bobby C. hesitated. He tried to glance over at Tony but Double J. was jammed between them. He changed gears.

Suddenly, Double J. reached out, grabbed the steering wheel, spun it sharply to the left and slammed his foot on the accelerator pedal.

"Jesus!" Joey hollered.

The car jumped the sidewalk, shattered the plate glass window of the Barracudas' club house and plowed right into the storefront room.

For a moment, they sat stunned and frozen in the car, staring out at the frenzy they'd caused as if they were at a drive-in movie.

The center of the room had been cleared for dancing. The lights had been dimmed except for one glaring lamp aimed at a card table in the corner where three Barracudas were rolling joints and drinking rum. They sat on orange crates and upturned plastic milk crates. Another boy was sprawled across an ancient overstuffed chair that had been pushed against the far wall.

A stereo was blasting out Latin music. Two couples had been dancing. The boys stood their ground glaring with disbelief at the car. The girls shrieked wildly and ran toward the back room, nearly colliding with a seventh Barracuda who was rushing out to investigate the crash with a palmed switchblade, which he flicked open instantly.

"Holy shit!" Joey shouted. "It's wall-to-wall spic," and the Faces sprang from the car; chains, bottles, knives, arms and legs swinging.

The card table was overturned. One of the rum bottles that had been sitting on it rolled across the floor. It was grabbed immediately by the boy in the chair who smashed it against the wall and waited. The other bottle had been hurled at Double J.'s head as he ran toward one of the dancers. The Barracuda with the switchblade jumped on Tony's back. Tony howled and whirled and the boy with the switch-blade went down and one of the dancers landed on top of him and then Double J. and Joey dived onto the pile.

The Faces attacked ferociously. Outnumbered, they kicked, smashed, sliced, butted heads, chain-lashed and ripped their way through the astonished and unprepared Barracudas. Blow by blow, they pared down the odds until three Barracudas had thudded to the floor unconscious. The remaining four were still fighting, but cut, bruised and sagging badly.

It was almost over. Bobby C. jumped into his car and started it up.

Two new Barracudas appeared in the doorway. One of them jumped into the fight. The other one spotted Bobby C. and rushed at the car trying to haul him out. Bobby C. slammed the Chevy into reverse and pulled away at full speed.

Three badly injured Barracudas dropped out of the fight just as the newcomers joined in. The Faces continued on blindly until, exhausted beyond will power, they began to look for a way out. That was when they discovered, one by one, that there was nothing but an enormous hole in the window where Bobby C.'s car had been.

"Get the fuck out," Tony shouted.

Joey's face was bloody. One of his eyes was puffed closed and practically sealed with blood. "Bobby C. chickened," Joey gasped. He stood, paralyzed, staring at the empty smashed window.

Double J. threw a farewell punch that brought one Barracuda down and his dinner up. Then he grabbed Joey. "I got him," he yelled to Tony. "Come on!"

No one chased them as they skittered through the glass on the sidewalk. They limped and puffed and dragged themselves to the corner. There was no sign of Bobby C.

"We did it!" Joey laughed. His shoulders felt massive, meaty. His neck felt thick. His eye was

throbbing. He wondered if he looked like he felt—
like the poster of *Rocky*.

"Yeah, now all we've got to do is get the hell out
of here," Double J. said.

They looked for the car.

"Man, he really chickened!"

"Let's go." Tony looked at Joey. "You can make it."

"No problem," Joey grinned.

They whipped around the corner and down a
side street. Suddenly, Bobby C.'s car appeared coming at them from the other direction. The old Chevy
snapped into a tight U-turn and screeched to a stop
beside them. The Faces stared at the car.

"Come on," Bobby C. hollered.

They hesitated for a moment, then piled in. No
one said anything to Bobby C. Their faces were
grim whenever they glanced at him. Their anger was
multiplied by knowledge that the silent tension and
hostility in the car was eating away their triumph.
They occupied themselves with checking their
wounds, touching the sore and kicked raw patches,
looking for blood, wiping and binding cuts.

"Nothing broken," Joey said. He'd meant to express joy; it came out flat, dispirited. "Fucking mira-
cle," he mumbled tiredly.

The break in the silence tempted Bobby C. "I was
driving around . . . looking for you," he said weakly.

There was no response. He glanced at them;
quickly over his shoulder at Double J. and Joey, then
at Tony, who turned and stared out the window. Fear
and disgrace drew a heavy sigh from Bobby C., a sigh
so heavy it might have been a moan. He drove on
silently. Without asking where they wanted to go or
what to do next, he drove them each home and each
one of them got out of the car without looking at him.

Tony was the last to go.

"We going to see Gus tomorrow?" Bobby C. asked
as Tony opened the door.

"Got no time. Maybe Saturday."

"Saturday's the Sweepstakes, ain't it?" Bobby C.'s
enthusiasm was forced and awkward.

"Yeah," Tony said, and got out of the car and walked away.

Bobby C. didn't see him again until Saturday evening. He didn't see any of the Faces. On Saturday, he scrubbed the grease of the repair shop out from under his fingernails, left the top two buttons on his body shirt open and rubbed the little twisted gold horn he wore around his neck for luck.

"You look nice," his mother said.

"Might as well," his father snorted. "You ain't gonna have the time or money to, come next month. You taking Pauline?"

"I'm going over to the hospital with the guys to visit Gus."

"Lookit your eye, you could use a doctor yourself," his mother said. "You not going to the dance place?"

"After."

"So how come you ain't taking Pauline?"

"Berto, please," his mother said. "She ain't supposed to dance, you know that. 'N anyway, you seen what hangs out around there. Nice girls don't go there."

"What're you kidding?" his father said to her. Then, to Bobby C., "You ain't going to be doing much dancing anymore, either. Would a been better off if you'd a stuck to dancing, you get my meaning?"

"I'm late," he said. He left by the kitchen door, carrying his leather jacket. He tossed the jacket onto the front seat of the Chevy and slid in behind the wheel. He started the motor up and reached for the brake lock but didn't release it. Instead, he let his head slump onto the steering wheel and just hung there, slumped forward, staring at his feet through the wheel, at the polished boots with the two-inch heels that had cost a couple of week's salary.

He sat that way until his father stormed out of the house and banged on the window of the Chevy. "What're you crazy? You're stinking up the whole block. You could kill yourself that way. Open a window or something. And if you're going, go. What're you sitting in a driveway with the motor on?"

Bobby C. released the brake, backed out, and drove directly to the hospital.

Visiting hour was almost over. The Faces were gathered around Gus's bed when Bobby C. got there. Gus was beaming with pleasure. His leg was in traction, suspended by pulleys over the bed. Except for that, he looked healthier than any of them. Double J.'s face was bruised. There was a scab on his cheekbone and a fair-sized purple welt on his forehead. Tony had a couple of red scratches on his face. Joey's eye was in much worse shape than Bobby C.'s. It wasn't just discolored, it was puffed half-shut.

"You really kicked their asses, huh?" Gus was saying.

"Fucked 'em where they breathe," Joey laughed.

"Outasight!" The smile was still on Gus's face, but uncertainty had begun to wilt it. "You know . . ." he began. "Aw fuck it."

"What's up?" Double J. asked.

"Well, I . . . I been thinking, you know. I been in here now and I been thinking I ain't so sure."

"Sure of what?"

"That it was them, The Barracudas."

"What?" Tony shouted.

"What the fuck!" Double J. was stunned. "What the fuck you telling me?"

"You said it was," Joey said.

"I said . . . I said . . . 'probably.'"

"Right . . ." Double J.'s voice was controlled, coaxing. "You said it probably was."

"I said 'probably,'" Gus explained, "because I wasn't sure. Could have been The Spanish Barons."

"Shit!" Bobby C. marvelled. "What'd you do that for? We could have got our heads busted, man. You don't go in slamming no one up against the wall in their own club house for nothing. Oh shit, we probably *gonna* get our fucking heads busted now."

"Not you, lover," Double J. hissed.

Bobby C.'s eyes snapped open. He gaped in shock at Double J. "What're you saying, man? He lied . . ."

Double J. turned away.

Bobby C. looked frantically from Double J. to Joey seeking support, seeking relief from Double J.'s contempt. There was none. He turned to Tony. Tony looked away. Bobby C.'s eyes fairly widened with horror at the unanimous condemnation. He turned his back on them and walked out of the room.

"Look, I had to say something," Gus said as soon as Bobby C. was gone. "I mean we had to hit on somebody for it, right? Somebody had to get it. If I said I didn't know, wasn't sure, nobody was going to get it and they would have gotten off."

Tony and Joey stared at him grimly. Double J. shifted uneasily. He walked to the window, looked down at the parking lot, came back to the bed. His hands were clenched at his side. Finally, he turned to Joey.

"You remember how you were riding me the other night? How you said how I ain't got faith in no one. Don't trust no one . . ." He looked deliberately from Joey to Gus. "You were right," he said and walked out.

"I'd like to break your broken leg," Tony said.

"Tony, they jumped me. You were even there— wasn't five minutes later. They jumped all over me. Three of them. Lot of them. I had my hands full."

"Fuck you, too, Gus," Joey said.

They left him and caught up with Double J. at the elevator. Bobby C. was waiting on the main floor. He joined them silently and they walked to the street together.

"I could have killed him," Bobby C. said as they approached the parking lot.

Joey glanced at him. "You couldn't kill a fucking crablice."

Bobby C. kept walking. A few seconds later, he said: "What d'you think I am—a fucking coward?"

"What do you think?"

"Lay off," Tony said.

"What's bugging you?" Joey asked him.

"Something my brother said . . . about people jamming you into their thing; about trying to be something else. Fuck it, what's it going to get you, Joey—busting him down? He's got enough troubles. He's done."

"Hey, we going to make the disco scene early?" Bobby C. asked a little too quickly, a little too eagerly.

"I ain't going," Tony snapped at him.

"So how come you're all dressed?"

"Fuck you," Tony said.

"You wanna, you'll have to stand on line," Bobby C. mumbled.

Joey heard him. He started to smile, then checked the other Faces and decided against it.

When they reached the Chevy, they all got in without comment and Bobby C. pulled out of the lot and began driving aimlessly, waiting for an order or suggestion. When none was forthcoming, he lapsed into one of his melancholy stupors. The car was unusually quiet, as if by unanimous consent they had all surrendered responsibility, not just for the destination, but for the mood of the moment, to Bobby C. They were heading for the Shore Road when, with customary suddenness, he was alert again.

"My old man's nuts," he said without an introduction. "He used to hate Pauline worse than me. Far as he's concerned, Pauline's a cunt—*until* she gets knocked up. Then she's a saint. Don't make no sense. You know something, I think my father's nuts."

"I know mine is," Double J. said with disgust. "He's in a nut house to prove it."

"No shit? Thought he was in a hospital from drinking," Joey said.

"Was. Now he's in a nut house."

"You know," Tony said, "the other day I thought *my* old man was cracking up. He came down to the store, was staring in the window at me—only pretending he didn't see me whenever I looked at him."

"Why'd he want to do that?" Joey asked.

Tony shrugged. "This guy in the store said it was probably 'cause he was out of work. Anyway, he ain't out no more."

"Your father got a job?"

"Same job he got laid off from. Guess things picked up in construction or something. He got this telegram yesterday that he's back on."

"That's great," Joey said.

"Big fucking deal," Tony said. "He was so excited he squirted beer all over the kitchen. I swear. He hugged my ma and swung her around, you know, and the fucking beer sprayed all over the fucking kitchen."

"So how come you sound so pissed off?"

"I still got to put my money into the house. I said, what the hell for—your old age?" Tony looked at Double J. "He says we've got to get the savings account back up. Shit. Can't win. Cannot fucking win. Here, a year I've been supporting the whole house . . . except for his union pension shit. He's going back to work. I'm still supposed to support them."

"Hey, where are you going?" Double J. asked Bobby C.

"The bridge, maybe . . ."

"Later," Joey said.

"Fuck it, let's go over to 2001," Tony grumbled. "Check out the Sweepstakes."

"You mean check out the competition."

"I mean check out the All fucking Brooklyn Sweepstakes, what I mean."

"You still in, ain't you?"

"I don't know. I don't know shit about fucking anything, man. Just let's go over there, hey."

Bobby C. started working back toward 2001. In the back seat, Double J. and Joey took stock of the drug situation. Joey had two joints and about six downers. He didn't know the names of the capsules; the large white pills were Quaaludes. Double J. had the ups, a handful of assorted pills and capsules he could identify only as speed.

"Go around a couple of times," Tony told Bobby

C. as they approached 2001. On the first foray, they noticed that the street crowd was extraordinarily full. It was early; nowhere near midnight, yet. The street outside 2001 was narrow. This evening, couples lounging against the outer wall of the disco and the cars parked at the curb formed a human funnel which fed into the entrance. The people nearest the door were pressed together listlessly. It looked as though 2001 was filled to capacity and no one new was getting in for the moment. On the second turn around the block, they noticed that some people were leaving. Three or four couples came out, looking sweaty and stoned and flushed with whatever excitement the Sweepstakes had generated.

"Hey, Tony. Ain't that your partner?" Joey called.

Tony searched the street crowd.

"No, man. Over there by the door. She just poked her head out, I swear. Like she's waiting, you know, just inside the door."

Tony didn't see Stephanie.

"Okay, park it," he said, and Bobby C. pulled in to the only spot available, which was a proper distance down the block from 2001 in a no-parking zone.

The Faces got out of the car and tensed for inspection. Double J. spread the wings of Tony's polyester shirt collar over his jacket top. "Looking fine," he said, smoothing the shiny fabric delicately with his raw-looking fighter's hands.

Joey flicked Bobby C.'s gold horn and opened the third button of his shirt. "A'right!"

"For luck, hey," Tony laughed and rubbed the purple bruise on Double J.s' forehead.

Double J. winced. "Yeah," he grinned. "Try getting through life with nothing rougher to show for it than a lump like this one, hey. Just try it."

"Whatsa matter, you don't like my eye?" Joey laughed.

"You and Bobby C., don't stand too close together. Someone'll take you for one of them bears."

"Pandas."

"Yeah, pansy bears."

Joey jabbed at Double J.'s arm. "A'right, a'right! Let's go."

"Make way!" Bobby C. called, until Tony slammed his back.

"Hey, cool it, huh. A little style, man." Tony said.

They walked leisurely through the center of the funnel and single filed through the entrance door. Stephanie was waiting inside.

"Go on ahead," Tony told the Faces.

"Hey, Stephanie." Bobby C. waved to her. The Faces went on down the steps through the crowd, over to the ticket seller's table.

Tony was watching her warily. She looked at the scratches on his cheek. "What happened to you?" she asked.

"Shaving."

"With a switchblade?"

"Yeah. Whaddya doing here?"

"Same as you, I guess," she smiled.

He took her arm and led her through the crowd into the jammed ballroom. The excitement in the room was even headier than the usual supercharged Saturday night feeling. The aisles, as well as the tables, were packed. Standing people seemed to fill every available foot of space around the dance floor. There were a number of blacks and Puerto Ricans sprinkled through the crowd; their presence added an unfamiliar, festive flavor, provocative and spicy. There seemed to be a great deal of noise, but the music was no louder than usual and the people, if anything, were quieter. Very few were talking. Almost everyone was intently watching the single couple on the dance floor.

The Faces were in the process of evicting a group of local squatters from their table.

"Yeah, yeah," Double J. was saying, "you just keeping the seats warm, right."

"Really 'preciate it." Joey grinned as the locals squeezed past them, out of the booth and into the already jammed aisle.

Stephanie and Tony sat down just as the couple

on the floor finished their dance with a lively flourish to loud cheering and applause.

"That was Barbara Falco and Tommy Connors, number four on our list of disco dynamite making the decision even tougher for our judges!" Bernie's voice crackled through the speakers. "Next on the agenda of hustling hustlers is Shirley Charles and Chester Brinson!"

A black couple ran onto the dance floor. They were about nineteen years old. The girl's hair was carefully dressed to form shoulder-length waves and bangs that appeared to be shellacked to her forehead. The boy wore a flourishing Afro. Their clothing was appropriate to the occasion—flowing, stylized with just a hint of flash, and obviously color-coordinated. They were both dressed in shades of blue with green stripes, prints and accessories.

"Hey, Joey," Bobby C. said, as the applause ebbed and the dancing began. "Ain't you got that same shirt?"

"Whyn't you just keep on scribbling with your mouth shut. Fuckin' contest," Joey grumbled. "They let everybody in here. Blackies, brownies."

"Even Annette," Double J. said, as Annette drifted over to the table and stood gazing down at Tony.

Her smile was drug-enraptured. She stood unsteadily. She forced her gaze from Tony to Stephanie whom she studied with ingenuous jealousy. Her smile faded and her eyes narrowed and her stare became so intense that she almost followed it into Stephanie's face, weaving forward dangerously.

Tony glared at her.

"Hi," Annette said, screwing her flexible face into an exaggerated pout.

Irritated, Tony turned away from her. She stood, staring, weaving forward and back, silently waiting.

Suddenly he stood up and left the table—at a pace that made it impossible for Annette to follow him. She fell into the seat he'd vacated and slowly pointed her pout toward Joey. Stephanie watched Tony disappear into the crowd. A few seconds later, she left the table to find him.

He was sitting at the bar. She pushed her way through to him, her face mirrored his anxiety.

"Don't worry," he said, "I ain't having a drink. All I'm going to do is look at it . . . sip it a bit."

"I get high just looking at the bottles. You look edgy."

Tony scowled at her.

"If you're edgy, you're edgy. Nothing wrong with being edgy. Just admit it."

"Shut up, I ain't edgy!" he shouted. "And anyway, we didn't practice enough."

She nodded her head, confirming her diagnosis. "You're edgy," she said.

"Aw fuck! You want a drink?"

"I just want to dance."

"Then how come you messed up rehearsals?"

"I messed up what?"

"You were dancing with Pete . . ."

"I seem to remember."

"I can't dance with a girl who . . . shit, you know. I . . . Nevermind. I think we're on one after next— or the next one."

"Lucky seven," she said. "One after next."

They waited in the bar until the applause indicated that the black couple was finished and the next contestants were launched by Bernie. Then, Tony pushed the drink away from him and turned on the bar stool. Without speaking, Stephanie took his hand.

Her touch was cool and sure and he felt, suddenly, awkward about her having initiated the move. He let his hand rest limply in hers, until she started to release it. Then he tightened his grip. He took her hand firmly, gratefully, hopped off the stool and forced a way through the crowd for them.

They stood at the edge of the dance floor watching the lights revolve and blink, a checkerboard rainbow. They stared at the feet of the dancers slic-

ing silhouettes through the rainbow; sliding to the
melody, tapping out calculated hesitations to the
beat. They saw the music end before they heard it.
They saw the couple's final whirl and knew, instinctively, that it was final before it wound down to the
last melody line.

There were a few seconds of tense silence in
which the dazed dancers glanced around, from the
crowd to the DJ's booth. Bernie thanked them for
their dazzling display of disco daring and Couple
#6 acknowledged their applause with grateful,
breathless smiles, looked at one another happily for a
last moment and ran off the dance floor as Bernie's manic cackle introduced his between-the-acts
spiel.

"They were good," Tony said solemnly.

Stephanie squeezed his hand reassuringly. He
turned to look at her but she was staring straight
ahead at the empty dance floor. She looked calm
and ready and confident and he wanted very much
to kiss her. Finally, she turned to him. Her smile was
the kiss.

"Let's go," he said.

The music was disappointingly familiar. One of
2001's regular selections. Unchallenged by the sounds,
they began too easily, too ordinarily. They understood the problem quickly and, simultaneously, the
need for a fast, careful adjustment. They were moving with the music, simple and elegantly; but the music controlled the dance, not their own excitement and
energy. Then, suddenly, there was a tension between
them, a knowledgeable tension, that signalled the
start of a true performance.

Tony smiled. His face had been as mindless and
dull as their steps. He smiled wholeheartedly, joyously, and their pace and mood shifted. The change was
subtle, almost internal, but so radical that there was
an audible gasp from the crowd and a smattering of
applause from the most critical onlookers—the serious
dancers.

The rest of the crowd had been with them from the start. The less discerning audience had been content with their easy grace and physical beauty; had watched the dance as if it were a fairy tale romance being staged for them. Tony's smile was the only change they saw and understood and their enthusiasm quickened with confirmed illusions.

Stephanie and Tony were dancing cleanly now, floating, spinning, projecting images of freedom unbound and rapturous. They were both smiling openly, proudly, and only at each other . . . reflecting, accepting and performing the audience's fantasies. Their innovations became recklessly sensuous—too primitive for romance, too exquisitely refined to be purely sexual.

Annette, at the Faces' table, began to cry. She watched Stephanie and Tony blur: She dissolved them with her tears. She leaned her head on Joey's shoulder. He was intent on the dance. He scarcely felt the weight of her.

"You got a down?" she whispered into his ear. She ran her finger up his neck, circled his earlobe seductively and sobbed. Joey swatted her hand away mindlessly. Then, "Hey, what the fuck?" he said, and turned and saw her tear-streaked, smiling, pouting, drugged-out face.

"What d'you want?" he asked, startled; suddenly angry and shy and surprised.

She pointed at her opened mouth.

"I'll put something in there, all right," Joey said angrily. "Watch out who you're cock-teasing."

"Ain't," Annette said. "Want a down."

Joey, flushed and disappointed, glared at her. Then he shrugged philosophically and pulled a Quaalude out of his trouser pocket. He broke the pill, gave her half, wrapped the remainder in a piece of cocktail napkin and stuffed it back down deep inside his pocket.

"You want the other half, you seen where it is," he told her. He turned back to the dance floor just in time to see Tony and Stephanie spin to an abrupt and perfect stop with the last beat of the song.

The applause was immediate and enthusiastic, thunderous. People stood spontaneously to cheer them and those already standing around the dance floor and in the aisles, clapped and cheered and opened a path for them all the way to the Face's table.

"Okay, that was Stephanie Mangano and Tony Manero doing their dance of delectable delirium. . . ." Bernie bleated over the speakers.

"You got it!" Double J. jumped up to greet them. "In the pocket!"

"Wrapped and zapped!"

"Long live the king!" said Bobby C.

Annette stood and stumbled backward and watched them take their seats again. She moved slowly to Joey's chair and held onto it while Bernie introduced the next contestants. She stood silently staring at Tony, sometimes crying, sometimes just looking bewildered. When she looked at Stephanie, it was with such open envy that even her hate-filled face was pitiful and reflected her hurt as well as her hatred.

Annette stood and leaned and stared and cried and let the drug warm her until, without realizing it, she was rubbing herself against the back of Joey's chair, against the back of his head and neck and he, wordlessly, leaned back and provided the return pressure her body was calling for.

The applause for the next dancers' performance was loud, but not as frenzied or prolonged as the applause Stephanie and Tony had received. Bernie's verbal pyrotechnics strained to make up for the lack of enthusiasm.

"Brilliant and bravo! Glenda and Mitch, thank you! Thank you for the drama and the dance, the spectacular footwork and fabulous spectacle." He ad-libbed a malicious, drawn-out cackle, then got down to business again. "And now, from our cornucopia of Terpsichore—Maria and Cesar. Maria Huerta and Cesar Alverado!"

The applause that greeted Maria and Cesar's dash onto the dance floor was embarrassingly sparse. It came, too obviously, from a small coterie of Latins who had come with the couple. As they began their number, a discourteous rush of conversation erupted. People coughed and shifted. Ice rattled in glasses; glasses tapped the table tops.

At first, the couple seemed oblivious to the restlessness in the room. Their movements were confident and surprising, constantly excellent, innovative, perfectly timed and executed. Then, it seemed that they must have been aware of the audience. It seemed, suddenly, as though they themselves had willed the restlessness . . . relied on it as a secret source of energy which they began magically to capture, focus and use. As the room's attention closed in on the couple, their steps became more subtle and inventive. Nothing they did looked ordinary, and every move seemed effortless. They were projecting something more than romantic grace. Waves of energy and exuberance emanated from them—reached out and rippled through the crowd—and returned multiplied, to be processed in their imaginative skill.

Bobby C. laid down his sketch pad. "They're good," he murmured absently. Realizing his transgression, he glanced at Tony quickly, apologetically. But Tony hadn't heard. Like most people in the disco, his attention was riveted to the dancers.

"Jesus," he said, spellbound. "Look at them! They're so fucking good!"

Joey turned to him suddenly. "Tony?" His tone was almost pleading. Then, whatever he was going to say didn't happen. "Shit," he mumbled instead. "They're spics."

Maria and Cesar took their bows to deafening applause.

"No way as good as you, Tony," Bobby C. said loud and clear.

"No contest," Double J. announced, as if doubt and anger were the ultimate expression of loyalty.

Infuriated, Tony glared at them. "I don't want to hear that shit. They weren't just good. They were better!"

"That was Maria Huerto and Cesar Alverado doing their exercise in enchantment. Now—Janie Sparks and Billy Phillips."

Annette tapped Joey on the shoulder. When he turned, she extended her hand, palm up.

"You had enough," Joey said.

She slid her hand over his shoulder and down his shirt front toward the pocket. He grabbed her wrist and glanced over at Tony.

"Come on," Annette giggled in his ear.

He held onto her wrist and reached into his pocket with his free hand. He pulled up the bit of cocktail napkin containing the rest of the pill and pressed it into her palm and closed her hand roughly over it. Then he released her wrist. She kissed his ear and straightened up with a great deal of effort.

"They weren't better, Tony," Stephanie said of Maria and Cesar. "Different, maybe. But not better."

He stared at her until she lowered her eyes. "Bullshit," he said. "You know that's bullshit!"

They watched the last of the couples quietly. There were no surprises left. There was no competition left. Finally, there were no dancers left. Only the music kept going and the rainbow spray of lights. The dance floor was just a series of blinking colors.

"All right, folks . . ." Bernie the DJ shouted. He turned down the music volume. "All right, I have the decision of the judges. . . ." He pulled his mike out of its stand in the booth and, trailing the cord, strolled dramatically onto the dance floor. At dead center, he continued.

"And now the three winning dance teams. Please hold your applause until I'm finished. Winning couples please come up here as your names are called. Third prize goes to Sheila Larkin and Tony Alano. . . ."

There was a smattering of applause despite Bernie's request. Sheila Larkin and Tony Alano, urged on by their friends, made their way through the crowd to stand beside Bernie.

". . . Second prize," Bernie paused dramatically, savoring the moment, "to Maria Huerta and Cesar Alverado!"

Earnest applause and equally heartfelt hissing from the couple's newly-won and now disappointed fans greeted the announcement.

"They shoulda got first," someone shouted.

"Rip-off," a voice from the upper tiers called.

"You see," Bobby C. told Tony. "You're still the king."

Tony glared at him and then turned back to the dance floor. Maria and Cesar had run into the spotlight. Now, they stood, holding hands and smiling with quiet dignity, next to the first couple.

"And grand prize, the first prize, the prize that says you're the best, the top, the coolest and the creamiest. The first prize . . . goes to . . . Stephanie Mangano and Tony Manero!"

Bernie's last words were practically drowned out in the storm of applause and cheering. Tony sat perfectly still. Finally, he stood, unsmiling, and led Stephanie through the back-pats, congratulations and I-told-you-so grins of the surrounding crowd. On the dance floor, he managed an obligatory smile. When the prize envelopes were handed out, he accepted theirs and bowed and smiled along with the other winners and, as soon as the applause began to ebb, he led Stephanie back to the Faces' table.

"Hey, hey! The winner and still champeen!" Bobby C. laughed.

"I knew it was gonna be you. Had to be. Nobody dances as good as you do!"

"Really great! Never seen you lookin so good!"

Tony looked at each of the Faces in turn. There was an uneasiness in their manner, a forced heartiness to their congratulations. Furious and disgusted, he shook his head.

"You know who should have won. You guys ain't

blind! Come on," he said to Stephanie. He seized her
by the arm and pulled her away from the table, out
of the ballroom.

"Phony bastards! Own fucking friends can't be
straight with you," he raged. "Jesus, they'll lie straight
in your fucking face. Know why we won? It was
rigged!"

They were in the lobby. A knot of people were
jabbering excitedly in Spanish accents. Maria Huerta
and Cesar Alverado were with them.

"Rigged!" Tony continued. "They want to keep it
on their own turf. Ain't going to give it to no spics, no
strangers!"

"Tony," Stephanie whispered urgently, "I think we
won it! Really!"

"You think so! Watch this."

He walked over and thrust the prize envelope
into the hands of the astonished Cesar Alverado.
Then he rudely pulled Stephanie up the stairs and
outside. He yanked her down the street. She had to
run to keep up, to keep from falling. She stumbled
along beside him.

"Where are we going?"

"Goddamn it, good is good," he was ranting. "The
spics're good, they ought to get it!"

"Where are we going?" she shouted.

"Fucking hole, that place. It's like, it's like ruined
. . . hanging out, the assholes I hang out with, the
crap we do!"

He laughed in amazement, savagely. He turned to
her. It seemed as though he was staring at her, talking to her; but his eyes were glazed, blind. His eyes
were wide open. And he wasn't talking, he was dancing. He was talking disco sounds.

"Bump, bump de bump and dump . . . That's all
we do, go around dumping, dump, dumping our load.
Dumping on something, dumping on somebody,
dumpers in a dump! My pa gets dumped at work, he
dumps on my ma, she runs to church to dump that
and for all the rest she's got me, the dumper's dump.
The spics, we dump on them, they dump on us. . . .

Dumb dumpers . . . even the humping's dumping most of the time . . ."

"Stop!" Stephanie screamed. "Stop it. Now!!"

He stopped. He walked her over to Bobby C.'s car.

"Get in."

"No!"

"Get in!" he shouted. He opened the back door and shoved her inside. He took a deep breath of night air and got in after her and slammed the car door closed. For several minutes, he said nothing.

Stephanie had been afraid of him. Now she watched. And as his fury subsided her courage returned.

"We going to just sit here?" she said sarcastically.

Tony didn't look at her. He snorted ironically. "Maybe we'll make out."

"Come off it."

"You only do it in Cadillacs?"

"Mercedes and Jaguars!" she said. She softened. "Listen, I did my time in back seats. The Bay Ridge number, getting fucked over by some Saturday night macho moron. . . ."

"Yeah," he cut her off, "all the fucking guys you had, I bet! Maybe I *will* screw you."

"How?" she shot back at him. "I wouldn't do it here and you don't have a place." She looked at him. He was still staring straight ahead but her gaze made him turn toward her. "Even if I wanted to . . . which I don't," she added hastily.

"So it ain't so bad," he reasoned, smiling. "I don't have a place to screw you and you don't want to screw me anyway."

"It's perfect."

"I don't need a place if I . . . rape you." He was still smiling.

"Oh God." Stephanie sighed in exasperation. "If you intend to rape a person, you don't tell her in advance."

"That's the way I do it," he said very softly. He

reached for her and she pushed his hand away, firmly. He was tired of playing games.

"What you really been hanging around me for?"
he demanded angrily.

"Dancing."

He shook his head. "Not dancing. It's not just
dancing. You're a cockteaser."

"Don't you dare call me that!"

He laughed, surprised at her quick outrage—and
her naiveté. He had stumbled on a way to sting her.
He was not about to give it up. "Once a cockteaser's
got a guy's balls in an uproar," he said slowly and deliberately, "she usually splits. So why's a cockteaser
like you still hanging around?"

"You dumb son of a bitch," she raged. "You really
want to know . . . I've been using you! I been using
you to practice my act on . . . seeing how much I
could sell you!"

He stared at her, waited—one beat, two. Suddenly his hand opened and flew back. "Bitch!" he
shouted—and the hand, his hand hit her face so hard
that his own palm stung. The sound, like a whip
cracking, shocked him almost as much as it did her.

Her hands flew up to her face, protectively. He
reached between her raised elbows and began to paw
her. He felt her breasts wriggling beneath the sleek
fabric of her dress. He caught one breast in his grasp
and squeezed it viciously and was shocked to feel her
nipple harden in response. Aroused and angry, he
grabbed her arm and tore the neck of her dress. Her
free hand reached out to claw his face and he seized
it, too, and pinned her back and she screamed and
squirmed and tried to pull herself free but his grip
was unyielding.

"Remember," he taunted her, "you said, don't
ask, just do it!"

He held her arms wide and plunged his head into
her lap. He pushed his head down between her legs
and she tried to bite his hand but it was out of her
reach. She wriggled desperately but he forced her

thighs apart. He thrust his leg between them to keep them spread while he fumbled with his belt.

With one hand free, she tore at his hair. She gripped and yanked it with all the strength she could muster. When his head came up, he looked startled, as if he hadn't expected and couldn't quite understand her viciousness. She delivered a thumping kick with her knee to his groin and his face collapsed in agonizing pain. He groaned and clutched himself. Stephanie wrenched herself from underneath him and ran from the car, leaving him bent over in agony on the backseat.

He stayed there, doubled up, rocking back and forth for several seconds. Then, slowly, painfully, he dragged himself out of the car. Stephanie was gone. He stood motionless, his gaze remote, an icy anger replacing the pain in his eyes. He breathed deeply for a while, stretched, straightened and began walking back to the disco.

V

Saturday Night— Sunday Morning

The Faces, plus one, were coming toward him. The one was Annette. She was sagging between Joey and Double J. Her arms were on their shoulders and they were half dragging, half walking her to the car. Her feet tiptoed absurdly, barely touching the ground in their effort to keep pace with her body; to keep up the staccato pace set by Joey and Double J. who were achingly restless and high on speed. Bobby C. floated along beside them. His eyes—one, already purpled from the club house attack—were bloodshot and misty and opened wide with apparent effort. He was smiling and sort of humming and sort of dancing to some inner disco beat. And, smile and all, he looked quite ready to cry.

They stopped when they saw Tony.

"Hey, man," Double J. called. "Where the fuck you go?"

Tony's hostile gaze swept over them.

Annette tore herself loose and put her hands on her hips. She stood before him, swaying uncertainly. "I'm mad at you, Tony," she said spitefully.

He ignored her. "Where you going?" he asked Joey.

"Annette's going to give everybody a little present. . . ."

"Fuck she is!" Tony snapped.

"Am too," Annette insisted. "You don't care, anyway!"

He grabbed her by the arm and pulled her away from the others.

"Hey, man!" Double J. shouted, gripping Tony's arm and spinning him around.

Tony exploded. "Fuckin hands off!" He slammed Double J.'s face and followed with two more punches. Double J. reeled backward and Joey jumped in Tony's path, trying to block him, pushing him away.

"Easy! Hey, Tony! What the fuck!"

Tony ripped into Joey, slugging at him relentlessly, a machine-gun sequence of punches, out of control. Double J. moved in to help Joey and Tony spun on him and landed two more good ones before both of them jumped him and wrestled him to the ground. They pinned him there, kneeling over him, holding him down and staring, astonished, as he squirmed on his back.

"What's up you, man?"

"What the fuck you mad at?"

Tony, his spine pinned to the pavement, glared at them. Then, suddenly weary, almost dazed, almost as puzzled as Joey and Double J., he stopped struggling and shook his head.

"I ... don't ... know."

They stayed on the ground, the three of them, trying to clear their heads and catch their breath.

Annette and Bobby C. watched them apprehensively. Annette was clutching Bobby C. She was shaking with fear and clinging as tightly as she had when the first punch was thrown. Finally, Bobby C. loosened her grip on him and walked over to the other Faces.

"Come on," he urged. "We'll go up on the bridge ... like always."

Double J. got up and brushed some dirt from his jacket. Joey and Tony stumbled and wound up sort of climbing each other to an upright position. The

Faces walked quietly to the car. Annette ran after them.

"She coming?" Double J. asked.

"Look at her." Tony said with disgust. "Can't leave her here." He climbed into the front seat with Bobby C. and slammed the door.

Annette scrambled into the back of the car.

"Where are we? Where you going?" she asked as the bridge came into view.

"Up there."

"Could you . . . take me home?"

"After."

She'd been crying softly, all bent over, curled up in a corner of the back seat. Her eyes were still unfocused as she stared at the lights of the Verrazano Narrows. Suddenly she began to sob.

"Jesus fucking Christ!" Double J. shouted at her. "What the hell's the matter now?"

She sobbed uncontrollably.

"She's just stoned," Joey said. "Ain't you, Annette?"

"What a loser," Double J. sneered. "Ever see a chick get so fucked up she can't even fuck?"

"You so hot, jerk off!" Tony called from the front.

"She got me hot, she can jerk me off!" Double J. reached across Joey and tried to grab Annette's hand.

"Tony!" she screamed. She skittered out of Double J.'s reach and huddled deeper into the corner.

Tony started to turn, then changed his mind. "Cockteasers," he muttered, abandoning her.

"Your hand's too cold anyways." Double J. flung himself across Joey's lap and caught Annette's chin and pried it up and shoved his finger into her mouth. She gagged violently. "That's where I'm going to put it," he warned her. "Where it's always wet and warm." He took his finger out and she coughed and gagged and began to tremble uncontrollably.

Joey tried to put his arm around her, to comfort her, and she shrieked wildly.

"Hey, leave her be," Bobby C. said. Then, softly, almost to himself, he added: "She's a nice girl. Really nice. She ain't no cunt trap. Annette, you're a nice girl."

"I wasn't gonna . . . Aw fuck her!"

Annette sobbed and shook and curled tighter and tighter into the corner of the back seat, trying to make herself invisible. For several minutes, the sound of her misery was all that broke the silence. Then Tony turned the radio on and they listened to disco music until Bobby C. pulled over in the center of the bridge and parked.

The moment the motor, and radio, were switched off, Joey popped out of the car and onto the railing. He was tightrope walking along, arms outstretched and head tossed back. He was howling and walking along the railing blind. He stopped and bowed, theatrically, to Tony and Double J., then he turned and bowed deeply to the vast dark emptiness of the water twenty stories below and slipped or pretended to slip forward. Tony and Double J. watched riveted with fear, until Joey threw himself onto a cable and rode it to safety, howling and laughing.

Double J. took the railing next. He danced on it awhile, working up to extravagant dips and spins. He was gauging his chances for a cartwheel finale before moving on to the cables. Suddenly, a sound that was terrifyingly human but unrecognizable stopped him cold and he stumbled and leapt forward onto the bridge.

Annette had come charging from the car to the railing. The sound was her cry of anguish, alarming and immense as a siren's scream as she hurled herself at the railing and tried to scramble up and over it. For a crucial moment, the cry had obscured the act. A few feet away, Tony, Double J. and Joey watched uncomprehending while Annette began to slide over and downward.

They all moved toward her at once. Tony lunged forward first. He caught her leg, her ankle, as she slid. He held fast with all his strength. Finally, with Joey and Double J. helping, he pulled her back up.

Tony walked her to the car. "Fucking idiot," he muttered. She turned her head away from him and puked.

Bobby C. had been paralyzed like the others. He'd sat behind the wheel of the Chevy and stared numbly at Annette's frantic suicide attempt. Her safety released him. Suddenly, he jumped out of the car and ran for the railing in what looked like a parody of Annette's madness. He even screamed and his cry was not much different from hers except that he started to laugh as he leaped up onto the railing and his laughter broke the parody and the tension.

Joey collapsed against a girder and watched.

"Asshole," Double J. growled, and turned his back on Bobby C.'s performance as punishment for the insane second scare. But, when Tony returned from the car and began to stare, awestruck, at Bobby C., Double J. relented and turned to watch, too. "Jesus," he whispered, "look at the little fuck."

Bobby C. had been playing recklessly on the railing. He'd been leaping and twirling with far more daring than the others. He'd lean out over the water and pull himself back with breathtaking precision; and fall, only to catch himself in a monstrously precarious sitting position from which he might easily have slid off into space.

His timing and balance were exquisite—and utterly mysterious as he edged beyond daring. Except that no one could call the boy on the railing a coward. Tony thought about that. He looked over at Double J. and Joey. He wished Bobby C. could see the wonder on their faces; the admiration and fear he was capable of commanding.

As if in response, Bobby C. smiled slyly. He put his hands over his eyes, twirled and, as his face came into view, he lifted the hand covering his bruised eye and laughed. Then he covered it, and twirled again, teetering closer to the edge. He continued until he'd reached a dervish pitch and the bruised eye peek-a-boo became almost unbearable to watch.

"Hey, cool it," Joey shouted.

Bobby C. spread his arms wide. His uncovered

eyes were wet with tears but he was smiling. He turned away from them. He faced the blackness, poised to dive.

"Come on, we gotta go!" Tony called desperately.

"Knock it off!" Double J. bellowed.

Bobby C. jumped, veered sharply to the right and came within inches of missing the cable he'd aimed for. He grasped it tightly, dangling 200 feet over the water. He held on with two hands.

"Crazy," Joey said. "Jesus, he's freaky." His voice was a whisper.

No one spoke after that. They stood at the railing watching as Bobby C. began switching hands. His face had become familiar again. He was deep into his brooding melancholy. He was twenty stories above the water, dangling from a cable, dangling by one hand . . . then the other . . . then the other and he was absolutely unreachable.

And then, instead of just switching hands, he began to sort of toss the cable from one hand to another so that there was always an instant between grips when he had no hold. He was smiling, lost, floating weirdly in space from moment to moment, hand to hand, and then the cable was between hands. He was holding nothing and nothing was holding him and suddenly, silently he plunged . . . down, deep and out of sight.

An hour passed before Annette screamed. She woke alone in the back seat of Bobby C.'s car, screaming her way out of a dream of falling. The sound of the siren that had carried her from unconsciousness to waking continued.

She sat up. The car was parked somewhere under the bridge, near a gigantic abutment overlooking the water. The blinking red police light was real. And the boat searching the black waters was real too. The car doors were open and, outside, there were police cars and uniformed men and a huge searchlight being moved back and forth across the water. Three of the Faces were leaning against a squad car talking to a man in a sport jacket.

"You okay?"

She spun around. A policeman was peering into the back seat.

"You screamed," he explained.

She nodded her head, speechless.

"You okay, now? Mel," he said, over his shoulder, "she still looks kinda out of it. You think one of the medical boys got a tranquilizer or something?"

"You kidding?" A second officer bent down and stared in at her. "She was passed out from drugs to begin with."

"Mother of God, they're going nuts young. I'm going over and tell Harrison she's awake."

The policeman walked to the car where the Faces were standing. He said something to the man in the sport jacket who turned, glanced disinterestedly at Annette, nodded and turned back to Tony.

"So none of you guys think maybe he was trying to kill himself?" the man said.

Tony didn't reply. Double J. and Joey were adamant.

"Shit no. No way."

"Jesus, I told you . . . He was Catholic, for Christsake!"

The detective nodded. "And you?" He kept his gaze steady on Tony. "You're certain, too, right? You're . . ." He consulted his notepad. "You're Manero, right? You sure, too?"

"There's ways of killing yourself without killing yourself," Tony said.

The detective flipped his notebook shut. "Right. Okay, you can go now . . . all of you." He stuck the pad into his back pocket and walked toward the water's edge where one of the searchlights was set up.

The Faces walked quietly to the car. Tony hesitated near the driver's door. It was open. He stared at it for a moment, then slammed it shut and walked away.

Joey called out to him, surprised and hurt. "Hey Tony . . . ?!"

He didn't answer. He didn't look back. He walked fast until he got to the street, then he cut across it diagonally and began to run. He ran and then he jogged and then he held on to a metal bannister until he could catch his breath. And then he noticed that the bannister he was leaning on led down into a subway. He didn't bother reading the sign announcing the subway's destination. He walked down the steps. A train was pulling in. He jumped over a turnstile and limped to the far end of the station and got on board just as the doors slammed shut.

The car was empty. He leaned back in the seat and stared blindly at the advertisements across the aisle. The car was brightly lit. He wanted to close his eyes but was afraid that he might fall asleep. He wasn't worried about missing his stop. He had none. He just didn't want to sleep yet.

Several stations passed and then the train stopped. No one got on so he stayed. He stayed for three more stops and finally a couple staggered aboard and the girl actually gasped when she saw him. He didn't know why or care. He got off the train.

The station was a large one with uptown, downtown, local and express arrows. He chose an arrow randomly, by color, and followed it to a deserted platform. When a train arrived, he got on and walked from car to car until he found an empty one. Then he sat down again. A few stops later, a drunk and two very tired-looking boys got on and he changed trains again.

Sometime later, hours maybe, he caught a glimpse of himself reflected in the dirty train window. He looked gaunt and frightening and he could understand why the girl had gasped. He remembered showering and going over to the hospital to see Gus. It seemed like a lifetime ago. A lifetime . . . It made him smile.

Finally, it became impossible to find a totally

empty car or deserted platform. One or two people were boarding the train at each stop; morning people, looking sleepy but somehow fresher than the night riders. Some were carrying newspapers under their arms. The newspapers, thicker than the dailies, reminded him that it was Sunday. Saturday night was over.

Saturday night was over *forever*, he thought suddenly. And, suddenly, he heard the train. He heard its clatter and rumble clearly and he realized that he hadn't noticed the noise before. The noise had been obscured by thoughts he hadn't known he was thinking; by images and memories as random as the journey, by realizations louder and more relentless than the noise of any subway train.

Not only could he hear again, he could breathe and feel and think consciously again. Saturday night was over and with it the fear and anxiety of what would happen when the moment, this moment, came. It was here. Now. He was relieved. He was glad. He had spent hours and a lifetime riding underground, waiting for Saturday night to end.

Tony got up slowly and walked over to the subway map on the wall opposite. Beneath it sat a man in a jogging suit, holding a copy of the Sunday *Times*. He was probably in his forties and had sandy hair, a handsome, leathery face and a physique that reflected both the need for exercise and its positive effects. He was ordinary enough, except that he looked like a man who might be at home in Manhattan.

"What's the best way to get to the city?" Tony asked.

"Where?" the man said.

"You know, like Manhattan."

"Yes, but where in Manhattan?"

"West. The west side."

"Uptown, downtown? You're not sure, are you?" The man stood up and studied the map with Tony. "Look," he said pointing to a spot on the map. "We're here now. This is the west side of Manhattan. See, it runs from the Battery all the way up. Here"—he pointed to a station where several lines intersected —"this is Columbus Circle, 59th Street. Two, three more stops. It's the west side and most of these trains stop there."

"Thanks," Tony said. "I'll find it."

The light of day was crisp and bright when he emerged from the subway. He crossed the street against traffic and wound up running to a weird little concrete oasis for safety. The island, in the center of four different traffic patterns, was dominated by a large working fountain that sprayed errant mists as the wind directed. He tried to get his bearings. Nothing looked familiar. Then, he noticed the park off to the right. It had to be Central Park; it was too big to be anything else.

On some street opposite that park was the big brown building, the one with a name instead of a number. Nevada? Montana? *Dakota.* The Dakota—the block-long weird building with a name.

He crossed over to the park side of the street and glanced at the buildings on the other side. They stretched northward with dismaying similarity. They were tall, canopied, imposing. He looked back at the fountain island and was surprised to see a huge statue presiding over it. Columbus, of Columbus Circle. Well, now he had two landmarks in Manhattan—Columbus Circle and The Dakota. He walked north, determined to find it.

There were strollers out on the park side of the street, which turned out to be Central Park West, and joggers heading into the park and children and dogs. There were parents and governesses and young couples and middle-aged men in baseball uniforms lugging equipment and Adidas bags. He passed a few churches locked between the tall buildings; tall churches. None of them looked Catholic, though. Neither did their parishioners. Very few were dressed in black, hardly any looked uncomfortable in their Sunday clothes.

He spotted the big brown building four blocks ahead. It still looked like an armory to him. He hurried past it and peered down the side streets beyond. Most of them looked alike—skinny buildings, skinny trees. He turned into one street and walked to the center of the block, looking back and forth, uncertain. There were plants in most of the windows. Which plants, which window, which building?

He crossed the street and went into one of the brownstones. The vestibule was familiar. He checked the name tags under the bells. He hesitated, then pressed the bell above S. Mangano.

The voice came from a small intercom. "Who's there?"

"Stephanie, it's Tony."

"Go away!"

He pressed closer to the intercom, leaned his cheek against the polished wood wall. "Please," he said, "I've got to talk to you."

"You kidding?"

"I mean it. Please, Stephanie."

"Tony . . ." the voice like a recorded message warned, "I'll call the cops." A click signalled the end of conversation.

He tried the inner door. It was locked.

"Stephanie . . . Stephanie!" he shouted into the intercom. He pressed the buzzer for her apartment again, kept his finger on the bell and his ear against the intercom until he heard another click.

"Get the hell out, Tony!" Click, and she was gone again.

He pressed the buzzer and stopped and waited and pressed again and waited and listened at the intercom but there was no response. The hallway was so quiet he could hear his heart beating, too fast. He took a deep breath and another. He was losing the clarity he'd felt at the end of the subway ride. His senses were numbing again. The way his heart was beating, something about it felt like tears . . . like his heart would beat and burst and tears would pour out of it. He leaned against the wall away from the intercom and breathed and waited and less than a minute later a young man in jeans and a corduroy jacket came through the inner door.

Tony grabbed the door before it locked again and entered the hallway. The young man was looking after him suspiciously so, with conscious effort, he walked slowly to the staircase and mounted the carpeted steps at a normal, leisurely pace. At the first turn, however, he winged around the wide wooden bannister and ran. He ran up the remaining two flights and, outside Stephanie's door, he took a few more deep breaths. Then he knocked softly.

"Stephanie, please. Let me talk to you. There won't be any of that shit like last night, I promise. I'm sorry about that, Stephanie."

He heard her walk to the door. "You're sorry?" she asked from the other side. The genuine surprise in her voice made him feel suddenly ashamed.

"Yes," he said. "Stephanie, please. I've got to talk to you. I need to talk to you. Please."

"You need . . . you need to talk to me?"

"That's what I've been saying. Please."

"What you've been saying is you've got to talk to me."

"It's the same thing. . . ."

"Oh, no it isn't," she said and unlocked the door. She pulled it open slowly and looked at him. Her gaze was wary. "No funny stuff?"

"No."

"Okay," she said, and opened the door the rest of the way. "Come on in."

He did. Just that. He stepped inside and out of her way as she closed the door and he stood, unmoving. Stephanie regarded him cautiously. "First time I ever let a known rapist in," she said. She wasn't smiling. She walked into the room and leaned against the big Victorian sofa. Some of the cartons he'd helped her with were lying about. Some of them were open and empty; others half-unpacked. The dress she'd worn to the Sweepstakes was tossed on top of one. He couldn't see the tear at the neckline. He wondered vaguely how she'd gotten to Manhattan in a ripped dress.

"I'll just stand right here," he assured her. "You won't have to worry . . . about me jumping you or anything."

She stared at him curiously. "What's wrong?" she asked.

He wanted to tell her; he wanted to shout: Bobby C. is dead. But if he said that, if he opened his mouth with Bobby C.'s name on his lips, all the other things would come pouring out and she wouldn't understand it anymore than he did. Bobby C. is dead. He made a hell of a splash. Everything I ever knew went down with him . . . my brother's collar, friends you could count on, girls who were nice or not, faggots you could hassle, spics you could kick. He felt his heart starting again.

"Nothing," he said. "I . . . I'll tell you later."

"You don't have to stand there," she said.

Tony nodded gratefully. He walked into the apartment and wandered around, looking at the books she'd unpacked and the pictures—some already on the walls, most stacked on the floor near the fireplace. After awhile, he turned to her.

"I've been up all night . . . riding the subways, walking around. Looking."

"At what?"

"Looking, just looking. Stephanie, could I stay here tonight?"

"Tony!" It was an admonition; anger, disappointment, a warning in the word.

"No. I'll sleep on the floor," he explained. "Tomorrow—I got some money saved up in the bank —I'll get a room, something, I don't want to go back there, Stephanie. Brooklyn . . . I want to get out of there."

She stared at him wonderingly. "What are you going to do?" she asked.

"Get a job."

"What kind of job?"

"I don't know. Something. I'll look," he told her. Then he told himself. "I'll look."

"What can you do?"

"Nothing," he said. Then he brightened. "Nothing—just like you when you started."

"Damn you, I could type!"

He took the full weight of the reprimand. "You mind," he said softly, "if I sit down?" He waited until she nodded, then slumped heavily into a chair. He'd done enough thinking; he was burned out. Whatever she said, that's what he'd have to go along with for now. He stared at the empty fireplace.

"Tony?" Stephanie said tentatively. "Tony, I . . . I'm sorry, too, about what I said . . . about using you, practicing my act on you. . . ."

He looked up expressionless, exhausted.

"That wasn't all, wasn't it. There're lots of reasons, other reasons."

"Like what?" he asked.

She sat down on the sofa and pulled her knees up. She rested her chin on her knees and clasped her hands around her legs. "Well," she said in the voice he remembered as her Manhattan dreaming voice. "Like I always felt better when I saw you. I got . . . You gave me sort of like admiration, respect, support. I don't know exactly, made me feel good. I mean, feel good just being me. All the rest was like trimming."

Tony stood up. He moved aimlessly about the room. When he did speak, he looked out the window and not at her.

"Listen, Stephanie. Me being around, in town I mean, nearby. We could see each other."

"Oh shit, Tony. We had that out already, a long time ago."

"Naw," he said. "I don't mean that. I'm not like trying to hit on you. I mean . . . I mean like . . . friends. Like you once said. We could . . . help each other."

"Help each other?" she said scornfully.

"Sure!" He turned to face her. "You're not so solid about what you're doing, where you're at. You could use . . . you know, like you just said, respect, whatever. And me, I sort of think I'm not going to have it so solid either for awhile."

"Oh my God," Stephanie said. She started to grin and turned away embarrassed. "You want to be . . . friends?! You really do?" She stared at him, incredulous. Then she began to laugh wildly.

"Yeah," he said, smiling. "I do. I really do!"

"Well, do you think you know how?" she asked, her laughter subsiding. "With a girl? Could you stand it?"

Tony shrugged almost shyly. He had a silly grin on his face. "I . . . I don't know. Maybe. I want to. I could try."

"All right, all right."

She became solemn suddenly, thoughtful and removed.

"What's all right?" he urged her.

She regarded him silently, contemplatively. Brow furrowed, head tilted, she was deeply involved in some urgent inner dialogue. He waited.

Finally, with unexpected passion, she said "Okay . . . Okay, we'll help each other. We'll be friends." Then she smiled.

Tony grinned his dazzling lop-sided grin and rushed toward her. He stopped abruptly, self-consciously, a few steps from her.

"Okay, Tony?" she almost whispered. She held her hand out to him. He reached for it, hesitated, then grasped it.

"Okay," he agreed.

They stood together awkwardly for a moment. They looked at each other and smiled grave smiles. Then Tony bent his head and put his other hand over their joined hands. He looked so young that she wanted to hold him. She felt the warm, gentle pressure of his clasp and looked at his bowed head and, all at once, she wasn't certain whether she wanted to hold him or to have him hold her.

DON'T MISS
THESE CURRENT
Bantam Bestsellers

Bantam Book Catalog

Here's your up-to-the-minute listing of every book currently available from Bantam.

This easy-to-use catalog is divided into categories and contains over 1400 titles by your favorite authors.

So don't delay—take advantage of this special opportunity to increase your reading pleasure.

Just send us your name and address and 25¢ (to help defray postage and handling costs).